FRENCH CUISINE CAN KILL YOU

THE MYSTERIES OF ORVILLY
BOOK 1

Rebecca Dunsmuir

**MANDERLEY
BOOKS**

www.manderleybooks.ca

Rebecca Dunsmuir/Manderley Books
www.manderleybooks.ca

Cover illustration by Charlie Varin.

Other illustrations credits:
Apple pie © Can Stock Photo / Solveig
Typewriter © Can Stock Photo / Yaviki
Woman in chair © Can Stock Photo / Lenm
Hands on computer© Can Stock Photo / Kakigori

French Cuisine Can Kill You/ Rebecca Dunsmuir. -- 1st ed.
ISBN 9781723849367

In loving memory of R.

Acknowledgments

My warm thanks to Darlene, Gabrielle, Pam, Selina and Tricia for their help and encouragement. It is a joy to write, and a greater one to know that I entertained you, my readers.

Chapter 1

The last day of March brought a pile of leaves to the main entrance of the Greater Victoria University. They were swirling with the strong winds blowing that day on the rainy West Coast as students rushed into the hall to join the long line at the Registrar's Office. And it wasn't even open yet.

Amanda hurried to the building, holding tight the hood of her raincoat. When she saw the wave of future undergraduates, she felt tempted to turn around and go back to bed. Why do students always wait for the last minute to register?

Amanda opened the backdoor of the office and wiped her feet on the doormat vigorously. Kate was already at her desk, sipping a large coffee, a toddler's sock hanging out of her bag.

"I think you forgot something," said Amanda, pointing to the bag.

"Crap! Oh well, they must have tons of spare socks at daycare, they'll find one for Joshua. And even if they don't, this is how he spends his days anyway, one sock on, one sock lost. No big deal." Kate bent her head toward the large glass window and passed a hand through her short hair. "Have you seen what's waiting for us?"

"Unfortunately, I have," said Amanda. "I recognize faces we've seen a dozen times before. Always the same ones who don't have the right paperwork... So, how was my ratatouille yesterday? Did David and the kids enjoy it?"

"They loved it! I don't remember the kids being that happy to eat vegetables, especially Nathan who's so picky."

"I'll give you the recipe. It's very easy to make."

"Are you kidding me? Cooking isn't just about the ingredients, and you know I'm a real disaster in a kitchen. How many times have I told you that you should open your own restaurant instead of entering some boring information in old computers that crash all the time? You have a talent and you should use it."

"It's not that simple, Kate. What puzzles me more is that I have two degrees, one in psychology, one in French literature, and here I am, working in a registrar's office. Where did I go wrong?"

Kate chuckled. "I should've been the drummer in the biggest metal band in the world, and look at me, married with three kids. You did well!"

Both women laughed.

"Just two months left before you go to France," said Kate. "I don't know how I'm going to do this without you."

Amanda looked at her friend with a sweet smile. "You'll be fine," she said.

Amanda knew that Kate was more anxious about her well-being than having to deal with the crazy daily life at the office without her.

The past year had been very difficult for Amanda. Both her parents, who were in their late eighties, had passed away within a few months of each other. Amanda, their only child, had arrived quite late in their lives, at a time when the couple had lost any hope of having children. Amanda's father had been an only child too, and her mother had mentioned the possibility of distant cousins in Europe. Therefore, Amanda had felt very lonely through this hard time. The only family she had left was her friends and her pets.

Although Kate had been wonderful and very supportive, Amanda needed a long rest, and Kate understood that. This is why, in two months' time,

Amanda would fly to France and spend a year there, thanks to a small inheritance her parents had left her.

She had never visited France before, but it had been a long-time dream. Passionate about French cuisine, Amanda had registered for a very sought-after class with a world-renowned French Chef to improve her culinary skills. She had booked a little house for her and her pets in Nice, in the south of France, where the class would take place. She looked forward to learning how to cook traditional French meals to perfection under the warm sun of the French Riviera, and to saying goodbye to the rainy days of the Canadian West Coast.

The digital clock on the wall displayed the fated time: 8:30 a.m. Amanda reluctantly walked to the glass door to unlock it.

"Please, don't let the wolves in," implored Kate.

"Too late," answered Amanda. "We're doomed to live a life of endless registration, until the end of time."

And at 8:30 a.m. sharp, the 'big wolves' invaded the office and ran to the ticket dispenser. The number one appeared in red on the electronic 'Now Serving' board.

Chapter 2

A bit later that same morning, a mailman walked with difficulty on Bayview Road, facing into forceful winds. The heavy loaded bags he carried, filled with letters, flyers and parcels, made him swing back and forth. He was just a few steps away from the house at number 466, where he had to deliver a letter, but these few steps felt like an obstacle course. Finally, the mailman staggered up the steps and dropped the letter in the mail slot of Amanda's red door. A letter that would change her destiny.

Although the important document was delivered on time, Amanda would have to wait another day to read its contents. On the other side of the red door, a small, white, furry paw took possession of the brown envelope as soon as it landed on the floor. Bronx— the most unpleasant cat of all—was determined to make it his new treasure. This was the exact reason why Amanda had opted for email delivery only.

The day she discovered that Bronx had hidden away sixty-two letters in a large flower pot behind the old shed, Amanda called Canada Post to apologize for the many and regular complaints she had been filing for over two years. The agent on the phone was not impressed at all. What kind of dummy couldn't figure out that her cat had stolen her mail for that long? To be fair, this employee didn't know Bronx's twisted mind...

Carrying the precious letter in his mouth, the cat ran to the other end of the corridor and escaped through the pet door in the kitchen. D'Artagnan ran after him, barking. The dog wasn't sure yet why he was barking, but he knew for sure that this damned cat was up to no good.

D'Artagnan was the opposite of Bronx. Affectionate, fun, obedient. Most of the time obedient. And tall. Very tall. When the Great Dane stood up on his back legs to put his front ones on Amanda's shoulders, he reached an impressive six foot height. Amanda, who was only 5'3'', would lose her balance and land on her butt. D'Artagnan always believed that this was a game; Amanda did not.

Knowing that he couldn't get out of the house and run after this evil cat, d'Artagnan gave up and returned to his pillow, growling. His 'pillow' was a sofa, his dedicated sofa, that Bronx had no right to step on.

The dog mumbled for a while, devising a plan to take revenge on his worst enemy once he'd be back into the house.

After the last applicant of the day—holding the ticket number 302—was called and helped, Kate closed the registrar's door. Amanda was still rushing to enter some data into her computer. She kept looking nervously at the clock hung on the wall facing her. Twenty minutes left. The longest minutes ever, and one of the most painful days at work.

"No! No, no, no!" said Amanda "Don't freeze again, don't!" The screen froze. Amanda hit the computer. "Damn screen! I just said, 'don't freeze!'"

"It's just a computer," said Kate, "why do you expect it to listen to you?"

Amanda scrunched up her face. Kate smiled.

"Just leave the forms until tomorrow. Anyway, by the time you reboot the computer, re-open the program, and so on, and so on... it will be time to go. These applications won't go anywhere."

Kate was right. But this goddam machine... it was a curse. The university had recently installed new software to manage student files, but they hadn't upgraded the hardware. Big mistake. The outdated computers often failed to agree with the new software, which gave a lot of headaches to the employees at the Registrar's Office. What was supposed to make their lives easier and more productive had quickly turned into a daily ordeal.

Amanda put the paperwork into her drawer and locked it. The women turned off their computers, took their coats, and left.

"Did I tell you about this guy who wore a wig and glasses to file another fake application?" said Amanda.

"What are you talking about?" asked Kate.

"An idiot came in today and filed two different applications for the same program to try to double his chances of getting in. The second time he was wearing a wig and fake glasses. Unlucky for him, I'm the one he met twice at the front desk."

"Are you serious?"

"Very serious. Are they stupid or what? Can you imagine that these kids are going to university next year?"

"Well, maybe not this one..." answered Kate.

The friends laughed and joked about the students as they walked down the long corridor that led to the back of the building. They talked for a while in the parking lot and then parted ways.

Although Amanda was exhausted by this crazy day, she still had to do one important thing before heading home: a stop at the grocery store.

Chapter 3

When d'Artagnan heard the key turning in the lock, the dog woke up at once and galloped out of the living-room, executed a sharp turn to get into the corridor, and slid on his rear end like an Olympian in a bobsled competition.

Amanda could barely open the door. The dog was barking, jumping, turning around himself, blocking the entrance.

"D'Artagnan, move away, please!" said Amanda. "I promise we'll go for a walk in a few minutes, but I need to go into the house first."

Finally, d'Artagnan calmed down, and Amanda stepped into the house. Her big friend jumped up on her and licked her face.

"Yes, yes, I love you too, d'Art."

Amanda patted the dog to help him calm down, but d'Artagnan kept blocking her way as she tried to reach the living-room.

"This is getting old, d'Art. Come on!"

Amanda put the heavy grocery bags on the floor and slumped on the couch. The dog jumped beside her and lay his head on her lap.

"My day was exhausting. How was yours, d'Art?" Amanda sighed and caressed d'Artagnan's head. The dog was looking at her as if she were the Seventh Wonder of the canine's world. Who could resist that?

Silently and slowly, moving with a dexterity that only a feline can master, Bronx entered the kitchen through the pet door. Not even a sound. His timing was perfect: Amanda was cooking and d'Artagnan wasn't paying attention to him.

The blue Great Dane was sitting beside his owner, focused on each little move she was making, wagging his tail. The dog knew that he would get a piece of the delicious thing that Amanda was cooking that smelled so wonderful. He didn't know what it was, but he knew that it would be tasty, for sure. What Amanda cooked was always tasty.

Bronx jumped onto the top of a cupboard to get a better view and dominate the scene. He was meticulously cleaning his fur, and his guilty paws. The—pretty much only—humorous thing about the cat was his fur. Bronx's back was black, but his head and paws were white, which made him look like he was wearing a black jacket. It suited him well because of his 'rock star on stage' kind of swagger, ready to dive into the audience at any moment. The audience being d'Artagnan, preferably. It always ended up in a concert of painful yowls, screeches, and barks. Not the sweetest music to Amanda's ears.

Amanda perused an old book whose cover illustration had faded away. The corners were worn out and the pages were yellow, some of them held together with tape. Why all this care for an old book? Because this wasn't *any* book. *This* was the 'Bible of French Cuisine.' Moreover, it was a rare original first edition of 'Je sais cuisiner' by Ginette Mathiot—*I Know How to Cook*—published in the thirties. A classic cookbook that has dominated French households for several generations. This was why French cuisine connoisseurs simply called it "The Ginette." Amanda had found the priceless book while wandering in an old books and antiques shop, one of her favorite activities besides cooking.

The irresistible smell of butter mixed with onions and bacon wafted throughout the kitchen, but d'Artagnan's nose was particularly captivated by the braised beef simmering in the casserole. Amanda grabbed a glass of red wine from the counter and drank a quick sip—it was listed as an ingredient for the recipe, but it didn't hurt to have a sample while cooking, right?—and she poured some into the casserole.

"Be careful d'Art." Amanda pushed the dog back and opened the oven to put the casserole inside.

Why would you do such a thing? D'Artagnan, looked with despair at the casserole that Amanda slid in the hot thing he didn't have the right to touch. Bronx smiled viciously when he saw the dog's disappointment.

"One hour, d'Art, and the magic of French cuisine will end up teasing our palates."

The dog mumbled and followed Amanda in the living-room. Bronx jumped down from his cupboard and followed them. With a bit of luck, he'd might be able to annoy this dummy dog a bit.

Amanda opened her laptop and browsed her favorite website, *allyourfrenchmovies.fr*. She was a fan of historical romantic movies, particularly the ones set in France. She had read a plethora of old romance novels—in French, if you please, this is how she kept practicing her second language—and had watched hours of famous French cloak-and-dagger movies. This evening would be the twelfth rewatch of one of her favorite classics: The Three Musketeers.

Amanda put the computer on the coffee table, started the movie, and sat comfortably on the sofa. D'Artagnan joined her, slid his head under her left arm, and put one big paw on her lap. Receiving affection from Amanda wasn't an option with d'Artagnan; it was a requirement.

"Hey d'Art, this is the movie that inspired me to give you your name. You were so small and so cute. Look at your big paws, now."

D'Artagnan raised his eyes to Amanda. *I've heard this story a thousand times, already. And we've seen this movie a thousand times too.*

Bronx was sitting on the armrest, on the opposite side of the couch. He gave Amanda a sideways look, not moved a bit by the evocation of this past event. It was a dark day, the day that this dummy dog had arrived in the house. Nothing to celebrate, really.

The opening credits started, accompanied by a dramatic soundtrack typical of these old movies that mixed adventure and romance.

"Look d'Art, that's France. A beautiful country we'll visit soon. You'll love it there because they make excellent food. What do you think?"

D'Artagnan was doubtful. *I'm perfectly fine here. Is the thing in the oven cooked yet?*

While Amanda had her eyes fixed on the computer screen, d'Artagnan began to fall asleep. Bronx knew that it was the right time to make a strategic move. Discreetly, the cat went from the armrest to the cushion located just behind the dog's back, and hid behind it. Bronx wasn't the least bit interested in horses galloping, men fighting with swords or women in beautiful dresses crying in despair. This cat's sick brain was constantly concocting Machiavellian plans to torture the hateful dog, with the intention of eliminating him from this world. Definitely.

Bronx had never been a friendly cat, and one could wonder why Amanda kept and fed such a pest. Well, to be fair, he had been a delightful creature for a short period of time in his life. Amanda had found the cat one freezing evening during the winter, under the front stairs outdoors. He was just a tiny, skinny kitten, crying for help with a weak little voice. Amanda had heard him and was heartbroken when she saw him. She couldn't possibly leave the poor animal out there. For a while, Amanda's home was heaven to Bronx, who thought that life would be forever sweet and perfect. Then... then, one day, she came home holding something in her arms. And when she put this something on the floor to show it to him, the cat nearly had a heart attack. Amanda had brought a dog home. *A dog!* An ugly, blue greyish dog, with big paws and a big head. And such a dumb look!

"Oh, look d'Art, that's one of our favorite scenes."

D'Artagnan opened one lazy eye. *We have favorite scenes?*

Two men were fighting a duel, crossing their swords, shouting, jumping on roofs, all the while smiling facetiously at their opponents. As the combat rose in tension and volume, Bronx slid his paw under the cushion and quickly dug his claws deep into d'Artagnan's butt, then ran away as fast as he could. The dog stood up abruptly, barking, and hit Amanda's hand as she brought her glass of red wine to her mouth. The glass flew away, pouring its contents all over Amanda's sweater, then fell on the floor, breaking into pieces.

"D'Artagnan!" protested Amanda.

The dog ran after the devil cat, barking and searching everywhere frantically. But Bronx had already taken refuge in a secret hideout in the house.

"What's wrong with you?" asked Amanda, rubbing her sweater with a cloth.

The buzzer went off. D'Artagnan, who was sniffing the bottom of a door, raised his head and froze. He knew what this sound meant.

Amanda went to the kitchen, followed closely by the Great Dane. She took a pair of mitts and opened the oven. D'Artagnan carefully stayed a few feet away behind Amanda. She removed the casserole slowly and put it on the top of the stove, and closed the oven door. Then she lifted the casserole lid. A cloud of steam rose up. Amanda sniffed the pot, eyes closed. She smiled.

"Oh d'Art, you're going to love this."

D'Artagnan wagged his tail in agreement. Amanda took a large bowl from a cupboard and put some of the delicious stew in it. She put it aside in a corner of the kitchen counter. "Just a few more minutes d'Art, it's too hot right now."

The dog lost his enthusiasm. *Are you kidding me? This is torture!*

Amanda prepared a plate for herself. "You know, you lucky dog, you're going to eat a classic meal of French cuisine. I don't know many dogs who get treated so well."

After a few minutes—that felt like hours to d'Artagnan—Amanda put the bowl on the floor.

The dog rushed toward it and gobbled the food greedily. *By all the dogs' saints, this thing is delicious!*

The dog felt something approaching slowly on his right side. A black shadow on the floor was growing bigger. In a fraction of a second, d'Artagnan extended his back-right leg and gave Bronx a solid kick with his big paw. The cat yowled and flew all the way to the other end of the kitchen.

Sometimes, revenge has the sweet taste of a good beef bourguignon melting in your mouth…

Chapter 4

After a good night's sleep with dreams of long passionate kisses with a handsome French knight, an escape on a horse, and cooking pastries, Amanda woke up at 6 a.m., as she usually did.

She slid her feet into her fluffy slippers, put on her long wool sweater, and went to the kitchen to start the coffee maker. While it was brewing, Amanda trudged to the bathroom to have a quick shower.

D'Artagnan followed her each step of the way from the second Amanda put her feet on the floor. He stopped when she entered the shower though. Bathing wasn't his thing.

While sipping her coffee and enjoying a generous piece of chocolate cake she had baked a few days before, Amanda checked the first emails of the day on her laptop—mostly advertisements for sales promotions from various stores that she preferred to ignore for the sake of her bank account.

"Look at that! Angie is going for a whole month to Guadeloupe. Lucky her... Did you know that they speak French there too, d'Art?"

D'Artagnan was unsure what that was all about. He just hoped that Amanda wouldn't forget to fill his bowl before she left for work. She put her empty cup of coffee in the sink, grabbed a plastic box from the fridge and put it in her lunch bag.

Me, me, me! The straightforward look that d'Artagnan gave Amanda should've sent an unambiguous message, right? The woman took another box from the fridge, removed its lid and poured its content in d'Artagnan's bowl.

Victory! The dog devoured the food as though he had been starving for months.

"Calm down, d'Art. If you eat everything now, you won't have anything left for the rest of the day."

D'Artagnan couldn't care less about Amanda's instructions, the dog was too absorbed by his favorite activity. Amanda walked to the corridor and put her raincoat on.

"Bye guys!"

Silence. Amanda sighed and opened the front door. She frowned. It was raining again.

"And no fighting today!" she yelled, before closing the door.

Under d'Artagnan's sofa, a pair of small eyes was shining in the dark, waiting patiently for the next opportunity to create chaos.

Chapter 5

"I'll never understand how you can eat so much and never gain weight," said Kate, looking with envy at Amanda's lunch box filled with beef bourguignon. "Where does all this food go in your tiny body? That's so unfair. I'll have to run for an hour just to burn off my salad."

Kate sighed as she planted her fork in a lettuce leaf. Amanda always had trouble gaining weight, a problem that many women didn't share with her. They would often remind her of this with unpleasant jokes. As a fine cook and a lover of French cuisine, Amanda felt lucky about this advantage nature had given her. But sometimes, she hated her petite frame. People tended to think that she was much younger than she really was, and they wouldn't treat her with the respect she felt she deserved. Wearing her light brown hair in a high ponytail probably didn't help, but Amanda didn't care about looks. A pair of jeans, a t-shirt and running shoes were her daily outfit. So, she looked like a teenager rather than a woman in her late thirties. Kate had often offered her to go shopping with her and do a full 'makeover,' but Amanda hated malls. She had always refused to be the object of a fashion experiment, like they do in these reality shows. She feared that she wouldn't recognize herself and would feel uncomfortable, or worse, ridiculous.

"Yesterday evening," said Kate, "David and I nearly had a heart attack. We were sitting on the couch and were checking the lottery results. After the fourth number in a row matched exactly ours, I thought, 'Oh my God, are we in? Are we in?' And... nope! Twenty-five dollars, that's all it got us. At least, it paid us back for the ticket." Kate sighed. "If you were to win the lottery, what would you do?" asked Kate.

"Damn, that is such a difficult question," said Amanda.

Kate looked surprised. "You never thought about this?"

"Not really... well, maybe I'd open this restaurant you keep nagging me about? I don't know. What would you do?" asked Amanda.

Kate grinned and put her cutlery on the table. Obviously, she had thought of this possibility many times and already had a plan in mind.

"I'd buy myself a trip to travel all over the world. And I'd stay in five-star hotels only. Alone." Kate put an emphasis on the last word.

"You wouldn't go with David and the kids?" asked Amanda, surprised.

"Are you crazy? Nope! If I win the lottery, it's time to celebrate and take care of *me*. No hubby and no kids. That's what I call *real* holidays."

Amanda wished she had this kind of issue. She'd be happy to travel with her husband and children, if she had any, but life had come out differently for her. She thought of her upcoming trip to France with d'Artagnan and Bronx. Although she was happy to take her pets with her, she also felt anxious about it. Amanda had never traveled with her pets, and never even had taken a plane on her own. Kate had offered to take in d'Artagnan and Bronx, but Amanda had shortly realized that she didn't want to be separated from them. A year would've been too long. D'Artagnan would be heartbroken and would never forgive her, and Bronx... Bronx would escape or make Kate's life hell. Between her husband, her three young children, and a demanding job at the Registrar's Office, Kate had enough to deal with.

The friends closed their lunch boxes and put them in their bags. They walked back to the office with a total lack of enthusiasm, knowing too well what was awaiting them. And they were right. The waiting room at the Registrar's Office was so full that several students had to stand up to wait for their turn. The lucky ones who had found chairs were sleeping on them or focused on their phones. The numbers on the electronic board kept growing by the second.

"Well, this afternoon isn't going to be any better than yesterday's," said Kate, rolling her eyes.

While taking her place in the booth and pushing the button to call the next number in line, Amanda's mind slipped into a reverie. She imagined herself walking along a charming French street, guided by the smell of fresh croissants coming from a bakery nearby. She put her hand on the door handle and was about to enter the shop when she heard "I'm number 158!"

A young woman was standing in front of her, on the other side of the booth, smiling and holding a ticket, relieved that her turn had finally come.

Amanda took the ticket the student was holding as if it were gold, and forced a smile.

"Let me guess..." she said, "Brittany Harrison, first choice social work, second choice sociology, you forgot your transcripts and couldn't provide a proof of address because you just moved here. Do you have all the documents now?"

"How can you remember all that?" asked the young woman, startled.

"That's the exact question I ask myself every day, Brittany," answered Amanda while playing with her ponytail with one hand, and typing the student's identification number on her keyboard with the other, "how can I remember all that..."

Chapter 6

His head stuck in the pet door, this is how Amanda found d'Artagnan when she arrived home.

"Are you kidding me?!"

The dog was barking, moving forward and backward nervously, trying to free his head. But he was so agitated that he couldn't release himself from his misfortune.

"Stop moving, d'Artagnan! How did this happen again? This is the third door you've broken. If you keep doing this, I'll have to leave you in a cage during the day. Is this really what you want?"

Finally, d'Artagnan's head came free.

"What were you up to?"

The Great Dane barked and looked at Amanda with desperate eyes. *It's this damn cat! He made me do it, can't you understand?*

Amanda saw Bronx through the broken pet door, standing outside by the shed, holding a white envelope in his mouth.

"Oh no, he didn't, the little rascal!"

Amanda ran in the yard. The cat let her run after him in circles for a while—just for the pleasure of being chased—and then escaped with his stolen possession through a hole he had dug under the gate.

"Bronx! Come back here! Now!"

Hands on her hips with an expression of bitter defeat, Amanda panted, thinking that she should visit the gym more often—no, correction: that she should go to the gym.

D'Artagnan ran outside and went directly behind the shed. A brown envelope was stuck between two flower pots, covered with dirt.

"Oh Bronx, you're a bad cat!" said Amanda.

D'Artagnan waved his tail. *That's what I keep telling you! Do you finally get the message? Will you get rid of this horrible cat?*

Amanda removed the dirt from the envelope and read the address in the top left corner. It was from France.

"A letter from France? What an odd coincidence, d'Art, we'll be going there soon. But I'm puzzled, I know nobody there. Who could this be?" Amanda walked back to the kitchen, followed by the Great Dane.

It was probably a mistake, she thought, but still, her name was on the envelope. Standing in the kitchen, she opened it and pulled out the letter. Although it came from France, it was written in English. Amanda's eyes opened wider as she read it.

She pulled a chair and sat down. Then she read the letter again. She stood up, grabbed a bottle of red wine, poured some in a glass, and swallowed it straight like a shooter. Her hands were shaking.

D'Artagnan was intrigued. He wasn't used to seeing Amanda acting this way and could feel her anxiety. What was wrong with her?

Amanda read the letter several times. Then, she took her phone and searched nervously for the contact 'Kate Batten.'

"Kate. I... I..." Amanda was so nervous that she couldn't say a word.

"You what? Are you okay, Amanda?" asked Kate.

"I..."

"Speak! Damn it! What's going on? You're scaring me. Is there an intruder in your house?"

"No," answered Amanda in a thin voice.

"Did someone steal something?"

"No, I..."

"You 'what?' Amanda!"

"I inherited a house in France. It says in the letter."

On the other side of the phone, a total silence went on for a few seconds.

"Amanda, are you on drugs or what?"

"Hmmm... Delicious! What do you call this, again?"

"Gratin dauphinois," answered Amanda.

"I can't say it, but I can eat it," said Kate, "good enough for me."

Kate had gladly escaped home, leaving her husband David with a crying toddler, a princess bossing around her older brother, and a young boy shouting in the house that he was going to kill his sister. Instead, Kate was enjoying a peaceful evening with her friend, eating her amazing French cuisine, drinking red wine, and talking about the incredible news. That was her definition of a relaxing Friday evening.

The women read again and again the letter that informed Amanda that she had inherited a house in France, and that the notary's office it came from had been looking for her for nearly a year. They would soon reach their deadline to find the heir or the heiress of the property, and if Amanda didn't contact the notary's office within two weeks, the old house would become state property, and she would lose her right to inherit it.

"This is crazy," said Kate, "you never told me you had relatives in France."

"Because I don't! I mean, as far as I know," said Amanda, still in shock.

"Obviously, you did. What are you going to do?"

"I don't know. All this is crazy. It sounds like a scam. Don't you think?"

Kate talked with her mouth full of gratin. "Don't know. But it wouldn't surprise me to learn that you have French relatives: you speak perfect French, you read French books, you watch old French movies, you drink French wine, you cook French cuisine to perfection, and I'm pretty sure that your dreams are filled with sexy French men."

"No—"

"Oh, come on! France is your dream. You must call this notary's office. You just have to check if they're legit, they probably have a website. If I were you, I'd be on the first plane leaving for Paris tomorrow morning to sign the papers."

Amanda pinched her lips.

"Listen, I know that you're in shock," said Kate, "but you have to go there and see this house yourself. Maybe it could be a nice vacation home, you know, where you could go during summers? Finally, your dream is coming true. This is crazy but this is awesome!"

"I have no clue what this house looks like. They should've sent a picture with the letter. Maybe it's an old ruin that's worth nothing, and it will only be trouble."

"If you don't call them, you won't know," said Kate, "and you'll always regret it."

Amanda pondered the idea for a while. She felt anxious because of the unexpected news, but it pushed her to do a quick check of her life: she was thirty-nine, soon to be forty, both her parents had died, she had no siblings, no husband, no kids, no cousin, no old uncle or old auntie, nothing. What did she have?

She had two pets, a few great friends, including her best friend who was sitting in front of her—eating her gratin dauphinois—a love for French cuisine, a few other hobbies, and a job to pay the bills that was 'okay.' Plus, she was supposed to go to France for a year anyway, so it was rather a good timing.

Amanda took a deep breath. "Fine. I'll call them," she said, with a twinge of doubt in her voice.

"Perfect!" said Kate, "now I know that I'll be able to enjoy French holidays for free."

Kate took a large spoon of gratin from the dish and put it on her plate. "May I?" she asked.

D'Artagnan heard the sound of the spoon on Kate's plate. He stopped licking the last bits of gratin dauphinois from his bowl and rushed to the table to force his head under Kate's arm. He nosed towards her plate.

"Hey, you!" protested Kate, "grow some manners, please."

D'Artagnan looked at her with innocent eyes. *OK. But are you going to give me your food, then?*

Chapter 7

Amanda eyed on her phone for half an hour although she knew that there was no point in postponing this call. Time was crucial, as the letter said. She had to do it. What was wrong with her? It was just a phone call.

So, she took a deep breath, dialed the notary's office phone number written on the top left corner of the letter, below the address. Because she was nervous, she got mixed up with the international phone codes and got the wrong people at first—she even spoke to a child whose language she couldn't identify—heard weird sounds when making other tries, and after the fifth attempt she finally got to talk with the right person.

"Oh, so you speak French, Ms. McBride? That's wonderful!" said the notary, Mr. Perrier. "It will make things easier. When can you come?"

"I'm planning on visiting France in two months from now. Could it wait until then?"

"Oh, no, Ms. McBride, I'm afraid it can't wait that long. It's quite an urgent matter, as the letter stated. You have to be here in person for the reading of the will, by next week the latest."

"By next week?" repeated Amanda. "I don't know if I can. I have to check with my employer, and of course, I wanted to speak with you first before booking any flight. If I were to go and see you, would staying a few days be enough to go through all the paperwork in case I were to accept the inheritance?"

"Enough? Well, yes and no, madam. You see, it's not a simple inheritance we're talking about. Sure, there are a lot of forms to sign and a lot of procedures to follow, and French bureaucracy can be slow, but it's not what I'm worried about. In fact, I'd suggest that you come here and stay for a while before you make any decision. I'd say... maybe one or two months?"

Amanda nearly spit her coffee on the letter. What about her plans in the south of France and the expensive cooking lessons for which she had already signed up? "Two months!? But I can't. Why would I need to stay that long?"

"Well, there are many things to discuss and you might need time to make up your mind regarding this inheritance before you sign any papers. This is quite an estate we're talking about, Ms. McBride. "

"What do you mean by 'quite an estate?'"

"Miss, you really don't know anything about this property, don't you?"

"No. And I have no clue who this Toinette d'Orvilly you mention in the letter was. Are you sure that she was related to me?"

"Absolutely sure. It took us a year to trace you, but I'm glad we finally found you. Miss, we're talking about something big."

"'Big?' Big like what?"

"Big like a… castle."

Say what?

"Miss?"

Amanda's head was buzzing. "Could you repeat, please, Mr. Perrier? I'm not sure I understood you."

"You inherited a castle. A château, or a manor, if you will."

Silence on the phone.

"A castle?" asked Amanda with a weak voice.

"Yes. And not just any castle, but a medieval castle that's one of the oldest in the area. It's part of the history and heritage of our region, you know. It even attracts tourists who like to stop by and take pictures of it. That's why I suggest an extended stay so that you can visit the castle a few times and get to know the area and our village. See if you like it here and if you have any interest in owning this property. It's a big decision to make."

Amanda looked at d'Artagnan. The dog was moving around her chair impatiently, mouth opened and tongue out. *This conversation has been lasting forever. Cut it short! I need to eat.*

"Miss, I need an answer regarding your visit as soon as possible," said Mr. Perrier on the phone. "Whether you accept to inherit this castle or not, I'm afraid that you'll have to come here to sign some paperwork anyway as there are other details that I can only discuss with you in person."

"Oh?" Amanda felt more anxious every second. "Well, Mr. Perrier, it looks like I haven't much choice then. I'll be there by next week. Where did you say it was located, again?"

"In Orvilly-sur-Mer. A nice little village in Normandy, by the sea. I'm sure that you'll love it. And you'll eat some good French cuisine here, Miss. Do you like French cuisine?"

Dumbfounded, Amanda looked at d'Artagnan. "D'Art," she whispered, "it looks like I have inherited a castle in Normandy, France. Can you believe this?"

The dog looked at her, indifferent to this last comment. *What does that even mean? Did you prepare food?*

Chapter 8

A manda was playing with her ponytail, rolling it with her fingers, turning her naturally straight hair into little curls.

"Normandy?" said Kate on the phone. "I know Normandy's famous because of World War II and D-Day, but pardon my bad geography, where is it exactly? In the north of France?"

"North-west," answered Amanda. She was comfortably installed on her couch with a blanket, watching a movie without paying much attention to it. D'Artagnan was lying by her side, and Bronx was sleeping on a chair nearby. The cat was snoring loudly, drowning the movie soundtrack.

"North-west of France? It's not at all what you had planned," said Kate. "You're supposed to go to the south, to Nice, right? What's Normandy like?"

"Based on the information I've found online, the countryside over there is quite green, there are many cows—apparently, really a lot—and culinary wise, the region is known for its crème fraîche, Camembert, apple cider, apple pie, and a famous apple brandy called Calvados."

"Sounds good to me! And perfect for you. So far so good, right?" said Kate with a lot of enthusiasm.

Amanda grimaced. "Hmm… Yes, but there are a few details that bother me: it rains there in a year as much as it rains on our West Coast, but without the sunny breaks. Apparently, it's quite grey and the days in winter are very short. Some people on online forums even described Normandy as, I quote, 'a depressing and dreadful region.' A person wrote 'besides cows and apples, I don't know what Normandy has to offer. Why is it so famous?' And I read this third comment 'people are awful there. They all seem to be in a bad mood and start drinking Calvados at 8 a.m. in the morning. Gross. Never going back there.'"

Silence on the phone.

"Ah. Bummer," said Kate, "but you can't believe what everybody says online. Some people can't help but complain about everything, these are trolls, you know that. Isn't there any positive things about it?"

"In the pictures, the villages look cute with their typical half-timbered farmhouses. There are a few famous abbeys and cathedrals to visit, like the Rouen

Cathedral that Monet depicted a few times in his paintings. And, of course, there are a few castles."

"Oh, by the way, did you find any pictures of your château, Madam?" asked Kate with a funny snobbish voice.

"Not so fast, Kate, it's not *my* château. At least, not yet. Strangely enough, not many. As it's a private property, people aren't allowed to get close to it. I've seen some blurry pictures taken from afar, between trees, so it's hard to figure out what the château looks like." Amanda paused and sighed. "Kate, it's not at all the dream trip I've been planning for so long. I was supposed to go to the beautiful French Riviera, to enjoy the sun *without* the rain, to lie on warm sand beaches, not on pebble beaches like Normandy has, to get a nice tan, and most importantly, to take this highly sought-after fine cuisine course with this famous French chef. I had to register one year in advance for this expensive course! If I cancel it now, not only will I lose half of my money, but this course won't be offered again until next year. "

"Amanda, I can understand why you're worried. I know, all this is unexpected and it changes all your plans. It brings stress instead of the relaxing time you were hoping for. Normandy doesn't sound as appealing and exciting as the south of France, fine. But it's still France, right?" Kate was forcing her enthusiastic tone. "Maybe this Orvi-I-don't-know-how-to-say-it is a quaint village with a lot of charm? I'm sure you'll meet nice people there. Not everybody can possibly be grumpy in Normandy. It's nonsense. This Mr. Perrier sounds nice. And they have good cuisine there too. It's still France! Right?"

"Right," answered Amanda with a subdued voice.

"Have you booked your flight yet?"

"Yes," answered Amanda.

"When do you leave?"

"In two days."

"Have you packed?"

"Nope."

"Amanda, I know you, please tell me you're *not* going to France with just a pair of jeans, an old t-shirt, and your running shoes?"

Amanda didn't contradict her friend.

"Remember," pursued Kate with a very serious tone, "France is not only the country of fine cuisine, it's also the country of fashion and elegance. Please, do yourself a favor and put in your suitcase a nice dress, a skirt, or a blouse, I don't know, something nice. Who knows? You might meet a sexy French man there. Even a chef, maybe? You have to be ready, you never know what might happen."

Amanda sighed again.

"Kate, where do you get all these crazy ideas?"

Chapter 9

Kate's daughter was riding d'Artagnan like a horse while her younger brother was pulling one of his ears, and hanging on to one of the dog's legs to keep his balance. Docile and patient, d'Artagnan let the children play with him.

Amanda was nervous. The Great Dane was enjoying his last minutes of freedom before spending twelve hours in a pet cargo crate.

"He's going to be fine, don't worry," said Kate. "You still can leave him with us if you want? The kids would be delighted."

"Thanks, Kate. But a year is too long. I'd miss d'Artagnan too much and he'd feel like I had abandoned him. It's his first time flying, he's going to be scared. I hate this." Amanda was pinching her lips nervously.

Two airport employees brought over a big crate. Amanda's heart tightened. She opened the crate door and put a blanket, a big bone and a toy inside it. Then she called d'Artagnan softly. The dog looked at her and at the crate. He didn't move. Amanda called him again.

What do you want me to do, exactly? D'Artagnan knew that the situation was odd. He was suspicious.

"Come on d'Art, go in the crate. Look, there's a bone inside, and a toy!"

You must be kidding me, right? The dog didn't move.

Heartbroken, Amanda pulled d'Artagnan by his collar. He resisted. Amanda caressed him and spoke to him with a soft voice.

"It's just for a few hours, d'Art. I promise that I'll let you out as soon as we land."

The Great Dane sat firmly on his butt. *You're really not kidding? Sorry, I'm not going anywhere.*

Amanda pushed d'Artagnan's butt. The big dog slid on the floor. Kate's children laughed. Their mother ordered them to stop immediately.

Finally, with great reluctance, d'Artagnan allowed one leg in the crate. Amanda kept talking to him while playing with the toy.

Is this the end? Are you getting rid of me? Why me and not him instead?!

Quietly resting in Kate's arms, Bronx was observing the scene with a sadistic pleasure.

Goodbye, dumb dog! Get lost in space.

Resigned, d'Artagnan stepped into the crate, and Amanda closed the door. The dog looked at his owner as if he were on death row. The airport employees lifted the crate and put it on a cart. D'Artagnan barked and cried. Amanda watched at the employees walking away with the crate with sadness and guilt.

Kate put a hand on her friend's shoulder. "Don't worry, he'll be fine."

"Well, it's time for me to go, I guess," said Amanda. She took Bronx from Kate's arms.

Wait! What? No! Not me too! Noooo!

The cat gesticulated and showed his threatening claws, making it difficult for Amanda and Kate to put him in his soft box. Finally, they won and locked the box quickly. The cat moved inside like crazy.

"As usual, this cat is a charm," said Kate.

"He should fall asleep soon. I hope. I gave him a sedative prescribed by the veterinarian."

"Good call! Your first flight would be a terrible experience with him awake. Passengers would hate you, and you'd probably never be allowed to fly again on any airline. Ever."

"Thanks for the encouragement, Kate," said Amanda.

Kate laughed. "I was only joking. All will be fine, don't worry. Go, eat a lot of French cuisine and kiss a lot of handsome French men!"

Amanda chuckled. The friends hugged, and Amanda walked to the departure gate, holding an animated and noisy box firmly in her hands. People looked at her, intrigued by the odd noise that came from the jiggling box.

Amanda turned around to have a last look at her friend. She wanted to say goodbye, but she could barely free a hand to wave to Kate and her children.

Chapter 10

After twelve long hours sitting in waiting areas, checking-in at departure gates, and boarding planes, Amanda finally reached her destination. As soon as the plane landed in Paris, she rushed to get d'Artagnan back. She opened the crate door with eagerness and anxiety. The Great Dane looked a bit dizzy.

"Hello d'Art, we have arrived in Paris!"

D'Artagnan jumped up on Amanda. They were both excited by this happy reunion. Meanwhile, Bronx was sound asleep in his box, tongue out and snoring. Amanda had given him another dose of sedative when she had gotten hateful looks and growls from other passengers because of the horrible monster in the box. She remembered what Kate had told her, and knew she had to knock the cat out. Although she had felt guilty taking such measures, she had been quite relieved by her decision.

Is he dead? wondered d'Artagnan, sniffing the box. *Good riddance! This painful trip was worth it.*

Amanda grabbed a luggage cart and put her big suitcase on it, and the soft box on top of the suitcase.

The dog frowned. *Why do you keep him? He's dead. My suggestion is that you leave him here.*

Amanda walked as fast as she could in the big and busy Charles De Gaulle airport, looking for the taxi station. There were several escalators above her, covered with transparent Plexiglas, crossing the vast space in all directions, taking thousands of people to their next destinations.

It looked surreal. Amanda had the odd feeling of being in a science fiction movie, a strange experience intensified by her fatigue and jet lag. D'Artagnan was still a bit groggy, but thrilled to be able to stretch his long legs. Intrigued and amused, people turned their heads to watch the petite woman with the tall dog as they walked by.

When Amanda arrived at the taxi station, she found a long line of people waiting for cars, all as tired as she was, some of them in a bad mood. It was already late and dark outside. Amanda looked forward to sleeping in a comfortable bed, in the hotel room she had booked. But for this, she had to go to the district of Saint-Lazare, and it seemed too far away at that moment. Both she and her pets needed a good night's sleep because they weren't at the end of their trip yet. They still had a four hour journey by train the following day to arrive at their final destination, Orvilly-sur-Mer. At least, one of them was getting some rest. Bronx had not opened an eye yet.

At 5 a.m. sharp, a cat full of energy woke up after twenty hours of deep regenerating sleep. Furious to see that he was still kept captive in his soft box— exhausted by the long trip, Amanda had left the box on the floor when she had arrived in the hotel room, and had slumped on the bed to fall sound asleep within seconds— Bronx kicked his box with all his strength, increased tenfold because of his anger, and slashed the thick plastic with his sharp claws. His paws forced the box open, and his legs came through. Amanda and d'Artagnan were awoken by a screeching box with four legs running in panic in the bedroom, hitting the furniture and the walls randomly.

"Oh my God! Bronx!"

Amanda ran after the box, caught it, and unzipped the opening quickly to free the cat. Bronx popped out of the box, howling like a demon, his hair bristled and his back curved, ready to attack.

Jesus! Is this what they call 'a resurrection?' wondered d'Artagnan. *I liked this cat better when he was dead.*

Amanda fell back on the bed. "For Christ's sake, Bronx, it's only 5 a.m. Our train doesn't leave until 10 a.m. I need to sleep."

For Cat's sake! I've been sleeping enough! screeched Bronx, *and I'm staaarving!*

The cat kept on complaining. Giving up on the last few hours of sleep she needed, Amanda stood up, walked like a zombie to her suitcase, and looked for something. She pulled out a small bag of cat food and dropped some in a bowl. Bronx rushed to it to devour the kibbles. Amanda did the same for d'Artagnan, and put his bowl on the other side of the room to avoid any incident.

The pets ate like gluttons, making a lot of chewing noises. But Amanda, who was starving too, would have to wait another hour to fill her empty stomach. The hotel's restaurant didn't open until 6 a.m.

Chapter 11

O h, my... Now, that's a train station."
    Amanda walked down the huge hall of the Saint-Lazare train station, pulling her suitcase on wheels with one hand, holding Bronx in his damaged soft box patched with duct tape in the other. She had wrapped d'Artagnan's leash around her wrist.

The station was bustling and crowded on this Tuesday morning. People walked fast in all directions, bumping into each other, which seemed to be the normal thing to do as they never stopped to apologize. Their only goal was to keep going wherever they were heading.

Amanda felt lost and overwhelmed. Her head was spinning. She checked the platform number on her ticket. D'Artagnan stopped abruptly, staring at a little boy who was eating a pain au chocolat. The dog pulled on his leash, and Amanda was dragged backward.

"Look Mommy! It's Scooby-Doo."

Amanda pulled hard on the leash. "D'Art, come on. We don't have time to stop."

D'Artagnan remained planted in front of the child and opened his mouth, showing him a broad smile. He should understand, the message was clear. Enchanted, the kid handed over his pain au chocolat to the dog. D'Artagnan gobbled it all at once.

Amanda turned green when she saw this. "Oh my God, d'Art," whispered Amanda.

The little boy started to cry. "Hey, why did you eat everything?" protested the boy. "I just wanted to give you a little piece."

The mother looked at her son. "What did you do with your pain au chocolat? Did you eat it all already? I told you not to eat fast."

Amanda felt terrible. In other circumstances, she would've stopped to apologize and would've bought the kid another delicacy. But she was in a hurry and she didn't have time to deal with this. She quickly walked away to disappear into the crowd, pulling hard on d'Artagnan's leash.

"You should be ashamed of yourself, mister. These are not the manners I taught you! And you know that you're not allowed to eat chocolate!"

D'Artagan was licking his chops, not caring a bit about what had happened. *Hey, these things taste much better here.*

Amanda saw the sign for platform 24 going to Orvilly-sur-Mer, and ran to find compartment 11. As it was in the middle of the long train, she hurried not to miss the departure. The soft box containing Bronx was bouncing in all directions and the cat was meowing in protest. With his long legs, d'Artagnan kept walking like a tourist smelling the flowers. Well, he wasn't exactly smelling flowers, but food, everywhere. He already loved the place.

An electronic voice announced that the train for Orvilly-sur-Mer would soon leave the station and that all passengers should get on board.

"Oh my God! Hurry d'Art!"

I don't need to hurry. You run ten steps when I walk three!

A man wearing the station uniform saw Amanda running along the platform. He walked toward her, grabbed her suitcase, stepped up into the train and placed it in the luggage compartment.

"Thank you so much for your help, sir."

Amanda climbed the narrow steps into the train. D'Artagnan stopped on the platform when he saw them.

"Come on, d'Art, not now, please!"

D'Artagnan hated stairs, particularly small stairs. And these ones were the tiniest he had ever seen. Climbing them needed some preparation.

Wait a minute, please. I'm still evaluating this move.

"Come on. Jump! You can do it," said Amanda.

Slowly, the dog put one front leg on the first step and suspended a back one in the air, unsure where to put it. Amanda pulled d'Artagnan forward. The dog was in! The door closed, and the train left the station. Just in the nick of time.

Exhaling with relief, Amanda turned toward the long aisle that divided the passengers' seats. *Oh crap!* she thought when she saw it.

The passage was not much larger than the train door by which they had come in. Amanda held tight the noisy soft box against her body and walked carefully down the aisle to avoid hitting passenger's heads, followed by d'Artagnan.

The travelers were amused by the intriguing trio, and some wondered what animal in the box could make such an unusual noise. Amanda found the four seats she had booked. They were facing each other, and would give her and her pets enough room to travel comfortably without bothering the other passengers.

"Come here d'Art. Sorry, but I have to do this."

Amanda slipped a muzzle onto the dog's head. D'Artagnan's eyes crossed over his trapped nose.

What's that for? I didn't do anything. Put it on the weirdo yelling in the box!

Bronx was moving in the box like a maniac, meowing with the full strength of his lungs.

"I know, I know Bronx, this isn't fun," whispered Amanda, "but please, be a bit cooperative."

"I can look after him, if you want," offered a woman in her sixties sitting on the other side of the aisle. She had grey hair pulled into a chignon, beautiful piercing blue eyes, and an inviting smile.

"I love cats. I can play with him while you take care of your dog. My cat died a few weeks ago, and I miss him so much. I'd be happy to entertain him."

"It's very nice of you to offer, madam, but my cat is not really... sociable."

"Oh, don't you worry about that. I've met a lot of tough felines in my life. I have the thick sking, I'll survive." The woman winked.

Amanda looked at the rocking screeching box in front of her. She felt exhausted and would certainly enjoy a bit of rest.

"All right, thank you so much, madam. What's your name?"

"My name is Liliane. Liliane Réjean. What's yours?"

"I'm Amanda McBride. Pleased to meet you, Liliane."

The women shook hands.

"I hear you have an accent, Amanda. Are you American?"

"No, I'm Canadian."

"Oh, your French is perfect, and your accent is so lovely."

"Thank you, Liliane. So, here is Bronx." Amanda handed the box to Liliane. "Please, be very careful. Believe me when I say that my cat is *not* sociable. He has serious behavioral issues. Don't let him out of the carrier, even if he tricks you into it."

Liliane took the carrier and looked through the transparent plastic door, tapping her fingers on it.

"Oh, don't you worry, Amanda," said Liliane. "Hello, kitty, kitty!"

Bronx calmed down and gave a killer look to the woman. *What you're looking at, old hag?*

D'Artagnan's eyes lit up when he saw the soft box in Liliane's hands. *Cool. Is she going to keep him?*

As the train left the station, Amanda settled comfortably in her seat and closed her eyes, hoping to enjoy a much-needed nap.

Chapter 12

Four hours later, the train reached its final stop: Orvilly-sur-Mer. Liliane shook Amanda's shoulder gently to wake her up. She had been sleeping soundly during the whole trip, and hadn't opened her eyes for one second.

"Amanda, wake up," said Liliane gently. "We have arrived. It's our terminus."

Amanda woke up slowly and yawned, stretching her arms and legs. She looked by the window. "Where are we?"

"Orvilly-sur-Mer," answered Liliane.

"Oh, wonderful, thank you."

Amanda stood up and took her coat from the overhead compartment. D'Artagnan was standing, waiting impatiently, ready to get out and move his numb legs.

"Oh my God, Bronx. Where's Bronx?" said Amanda in panic, looking around her.

"He's here. Don't worry," said Liliane. She handed the soft box to Amanda.

"How did he behave? Did he give you any trouble?"

"Absolutely not. I told him a lot of stories and he stayed quiet. He was real charmer. "

Amanda was perplexed. "Really?"

"Yes. Bronx is a lovely cat and such a wonderful company."

Was the cat dead? Worried, Amanda looked in the box. Nope. He was not. Bronx was very much alive, quiet and still, looking at Amanda with a smirk of revenge. This couldn't be good.

"Let me help you," said Liliane.

The women walked down the aisle to the luggage area, pulled out their suitcases and got off the train. They walked along the platform where the atmosphere was radically different from the Saint-Lazare station in Paris. It was very quiet, with barely a soul around. The station hall looked like a cute little country house. There were a few wooden benches placed along the platform for travelers to sit on while waiting.

"Are you here to enjoy some time off, visiting family or friends?" asked Liliane.

"No family or friends. It's my first time visiting Orvilly-sur-Mer. The reason why I'm here is quite an odd and complicated story. I don't know yet how long I'll stay. Sorry, I'm aware what I'm saying doesn't make much sense."

"No worries," said Liliane. "You don't have to tell me anything. A bit of mystery is always good." The woman winked.

"But maybe you can help me. I booked a room at The Little Norman. By any chance, do you know where this hotel is?"

"Sure. I'm going in the same direction. We can walk there, it's not far. It's the only hotel we have in Orvilly-sur-Mer, anyway. You know, Orvilly is quite a small village, less than three thousand residents or so. I know a lot about this place. I was born and raised here and worked at City Hall pretty much all my life before retiring five years ago. You can ask me anything you want to know about this village."

The women kept talking and walking along on Brigadier Street, the main street of the village.

Amanda was surprised to see how narrow the paved streets were. Everything looked so tiny compared to North-American streets. How could cars drive on such little roads? And the sidewalks weren't large either. Two persons, at most, could walk side by side. But the old houses with white walls and beams, typical of Normandy, were lovely.

Amanda smiled. For the first time since she had landed in the country, she realized she was in France. Her long-awaited dream.

Chapter 13

Amanda rang the little bell on the counter. A few seconds later, a short and plump woman in her mid-sixties opened a bead curtain and walked to the reception desk. She was fair-skinned with red cheeks. She wiped her hands on her apron.

"Ah! You must be the little Canadian? We've been waiting for you."

Why 'little?' wondered Amanda as she smiled and nodded.

"So, you're traveling with your pets?"

"Yes. Is it still okay if I keep them with me in the room?"

"Oh yes, no problem. We have a dog here too. Titi."

The woman pointed her finger at a tiny ugly dog with a ridiculous green rooster comb, sitting on a chair, resting on a pillow. He looked at d'Artagnan straight in the eyes, and growled at him viciously.

Gee. What's wrong with him? thought the Great Dane, *are they all like this here? I have enough with one psycho.*

"Follow me, I'll show you the room."

The robust woman took Amanda's heavy suitcase with a firm hand and went up a little staircase.

"Oh, no, you don't have to do that," said Amanda, "I can carry it."

"Nah! Don't worry. I'm used to it. That's my workout."

They stopped on the first floor, turned to their left, and walked down a yellowish carpeted corridor. The woman opened a door at the end of the hall on the right.

"Here you go, miss. I gave you the biggest room so you can be comfortable enough with your dog and your cat. What's wrong with him?"

Bronx had pressed his face flat on the transparent plastic door of the soft box, making his eyes look big and scary.

"Oh, nothing, he enjoys doing this," answered Amanda.

"Wow. Frightening little cat, you have there. By the way, my name is Régine. You'll see my husband Paul later. We're the hotel owners. Make yourself comfortable and call me if you need anything. Just dial 0 on the room phone, all right?"

"All right, thank you very much, Régine."

Régine walked away, then she stopped and turned around.

"Ah, forgot to tell you: we're in Normandy, so it rains a lot. Make sure to always have a raincoat or an umbrella with you before you go out. The weather forecast announced a storm for this afternoon. I can lend you an umbrella if you don't have one."

The woman went back downstairs, and Amanda closed the door behind her.

"Well d'Art, it won't be much different from our rainy Victoria, right?"

D'Artagnan was moving nervously around Amanda. *Nope. By the way, remove this damn muzzle from my nose. Now, please.*

As if Amanda had heard the dog's thought, she removed his muzzle. Then she opened the soft box with justified apprehension. The moment Bronx was freed, the cat launched himself like a cannonball and leaped about the room, emitting weird sounds.

"Oh my God," whispered Amanda.

D'Artagnan rolled his eyes. *Damn. This cat is crazy for real.*

Amanda knew that Bronx would stop his 'show' at some point. Spending so much time in a box would turn anybody crazy. So she decided to ignore his antics and make herself comfortable in the room.

The double-sized bed with a high headboard had a thick mattress that looked comfortable, and was covered with a pink comforter with embroidered flowers. A massive cabinet—probably a Norman antique—with mirrors on the front doors was placed against a wall beside the bed, and a chair and a small desk sat in a corner.

The room was big enough to allow d'Artagnan to stretch his legs. The dog was actively inspecting the place, sniffing every inch of the floor, trying to determine which corner was best to set down his headquarters.

Bronx jumped up onto the windowsill that faced the bed and walked along the three windows that overlooked Brigadier Street. Ideal for observing the action in the street or napping in the sun.

Amanda lifted her suitcase, put it on the bed, and removed her personal items to store them in the cabinet. It didn't take long: two pairs of jeans, a few t-shirts, a white blouse, warm sweaters, a pair of rubber boots, her toiletry kit and underwear. It was all she had brought with her. Her suitcase was mostly filled with food, toys and care products for her pets. If Kate were here, thought Amanda, she would definitely be horrified.

Then she placed four bowls with pet food and water on the floor. D'Artagnan rushed to them while

Bronx was still making a show of himself, looking at something by the window, making loud comments. Amanda took a quick refreshing shower and got ready for her important appointment with Mr. Perrier, the notary.

She looked forward to seeing this château.

Chapter 14

It wasn't raining, it was pouring. Probably worse than any rainy day Amanda had ever experienced in Victoria.

The notary's office was only a few streets away from the hotel, so Amanda decided to run on Brigadier Street as fast as she could. Despite wearing a raincoat, having her rain boots on, and carrying an umbrella, Amanda was soaked to the skin when she arrived there. As she pushed open the door, she thought that the shower she had before leaving the hotel might not have been necessary.

"You can put your coat and your umbrella over there, Ms. McBride."

A woman behind a desk pointed to an umbrella stand and a coat rack in a corner. The moment Amanda turned her back, the woman leaned on her desktop to scrutinize her from head to toe. Her head moved up and down swiftly, her long pointy nose seemingly acting as a radar. "Mr. Perrier will be with you shortly."

A few minutes later, a short and thin man wearing a well-tailored brown suit opened a large wooden door. He pushed back his glasses on his nose. "Ms. McBride, I presume?"

Amanda stood up and walked toward the notary to shake his hand. "Yes. Pleased to meet you, Mr. Perrier."

"Pleased to meet you too, miss. Please, come in."

Amanda stepped into a large office with wooden wall panels. A strong lemon polish scent tingled Amanda's nostrils.

"Please, have a seat," said the notary. He pointed to an imposing leather armchair.

Amanda walked on the thick red carpet and sat down. She expected the armchair to be cozy, but instead it felt quite firm.

Mr. Perrier seated himself behind the desk and put his fingertips on the frame of his glasses. He read the label on a file that was on top of a big pile on his desk, and opened it. "Well, finally we meet, Ms. McBride. At some point, I thought we would never be able to find you. I'm glad you're here. Did you have a good trip?"

Should she tell him about the psycho cat and the huge Great Dane she had been travelling with? Probably not. "Yes, very good, thank you."

"All right, let's start then. But first, we need to go back in history: Mrs. Toinette d'Orvilly died a year ago at the age of 93. She was your distant cousin, the daughter of a great-great-aunt, on your mother's side."

"Oh?"

"We haven't been able to trace any other siblings or relatives to Mrs. D'Orvilly or to Mr. Edouard d'Alban, her second and last husband. All the relatives are deceased, and the couple didn't have children."

"Ah."

"When we traced the family tree on your mother's side, we realized at some point that a part of your family had emigrated to Canada and had changed their name once they arrived in your country, which is why it took so long to find you."

"Oh, I see."

"Probably because the name 'd'Orvilly' wasn't easy to pronounce, the customs officer in charge of newcomers that day gave your relatives a new name. Unfortunately, it was a common practice in the late 18th century. Canada was already a popular destination for immigrants, so the authorities didn't take the time to think twice about it. That's why your mother's maiden name became 'Barber.'"

"Why Barber?"

"Maybe because the man had gone to a barber shop that day, who knows? Sometimes, the way customs officers chose the new names was completely random! Then, much later, of course, your mother was born, and later on married your father and took his name: McBride."

"I see..."

"Now, about the estate. As I mentioned on the phone, we're talking about a large property that has been in Mrs. D'Orvilly's family for several centuries. She took great pride in it, and took somewhat good care of it to a certain extent. But when her second husband died ten years ago, she lost interest in many things, including the castle."

"Oh."

"Now, what I strongly advise, Ms. McBride, is to go and see this property before you make any decision or sign any papers. Inheriting a big property like this one can sound romantic, but..."

Amanda was replaying a few scenes of the Three Musketeers in her mind.

"... in reality, it is another story," continued the notary.

"Then I guess seeing this property sooner rather than later is best," said Amanda. "I was hoping that you'd have some time to go and visit it with me now?"

Mr. Perrier checked his watch.

"We surely can. But the weather might not make this visit very pleasant."

It was still pouring heavily outside. The sky was hidden by dark clouds, and thunder was rumbling, getting closer.

"That's fine," said Amanda. "I'm used to rainy days. British Columbia's West Coast is known to be very rainy. And as I understand, so is Normandy." She chuckled. "I'm already soaked, anyway. I can't wait to see the castle."

"All right then. Let's go and see it," said the notary. He opened a drawer and took a key ring with dozens of keys.

Lightning flickered, brightening up the office.

Chapter 15

The windshield was obscured by the buckets of water that the sky was dumping on it, despite the wipers going at the fastest speed. From the inside, it looked like the vehicle was going through the big rolling brushes of an automatic car wash.

Mr. Perrier drove slowly, his nose close to the steering wheel, squinting, and constantly adjusting his glasses that kept sliding down on his nose.

"Ah, here we are," he said.

The car passed a metal gate and drove along the path that led to an edifice that dominated the landscape. A large and tall black shape got bigger as they approached. Mr. Perrier stopped the car.

"Ready to brave the rain?" he asked Amanda.

"I am!"

They stepped out of the car. Their feet landed in deep puddles of water that reached their ankles. Their boots got stuck in the mud, making it more difficult for them to run.

"Follow me, this way!" yelled Mr. Perrier.

Thunder exploded, lightning struck, and to make it even more difficult, strong winds turned their umbrellas inside out.

Amanda and Mr. Perrier ran as fast as they could toward the castle. She raised her eyes to see it better, holding tight on her umbrella, which was pretty much useless. She felt her heart stop for a second. Amanda had expected something big, but not *that* big.

The castle was made of dark grey stone, about sixty-five feet high and maybe a hundred feet wide. Two high towers at the extremities ended with pointy roofs, and the large windows on the front looked like giant black eyes. Amanda shivered. The place was grim. It wasn't the feeling she had hoped for when seeing the castle for the first time.

She and Mr. Perrier stepped onto the front porch, and the notary pulled the thick metal ring holding dozens of keys out of his pocket. He inserted one after another in the lock of the big front door and tried to open it. After several attempts, he finally found the right key and invited Amanda to step inside.

The big hall with a high ceiling was dark and cold, but at least they were protected from the rain. Amanda looked around, intimidated by the ample space. Mr. Perrier cleaned his glasses with a wet handkerchief.

"I didn't lie to you, Ms. McBride, this place is massive," said Mr. Perrier.

"Yes, it is," whispered Amanda.

"Follow me, we're going to start the tour in here."

They entered a large room on their right. The worn-out tapestry on the walls showed unraveled little threads and holes here and there. The faded red that once was vibrant looked dirty and dull. It was covered with a pattern of golden leopards. Amanda got closer and ran a hand along the tapestry.

"Leopards are the emblem of our region," explained Mr. Perrier, "they represent the British Kings of England who became the Dukes of Normandy."

Amanda turned around. Two antique chairs faced a large window, still bearing the imprints of their past occupants, and a lovely but deteriorated 19th century upholstered green sofa that had probably not seen any visitors for a long while was left in a corner.

"Is the castle all furnished with antiques?" asked Amanda.

"There are a few empty rooms, but most of them are furnished. I've been told that this room was used as a tea room when Mrs. D'Orvilly received guests in the afternoon. Very few though, she seldom had visitors. Please, come this way."

The notary walked back to the hall and went up a broad staircase made of stone. "I'm afraid that we won't be able to visit all the rooms today. It's getting too dark, and there's no power. But I can leave you the keys so that you can come back tomorrow and get a better look on your own. There are twenty-four rooms in total on three levels. It seems like a low number for a castle, but bear in mind that these rooms are quite large. It doesn't include the kitchen and the space in the basement though."

The thunder rumbled loudly, resonating on the castle's walls as if it were going to break it into pieces. Amanda and the notary hurried up to the first floor.

An old red carpet traced the path of a long corridor with five doors on each side. Mr. Perrier opened one of them. The door squeaked.

"This was Mrs. D'Orvilly's bedroom."

Amanda walked into the spacious room. The surface area was probably bigger than her entire house in Victoria. How could an elderly woman live on her own in such a big place? Mrs. D'Orvilly had grown up in the castle and had lived here since her childhood. But what about Amanda? Could she live on her own in the castle?

"As you can see, these are not regular sized rooms," said Mr. Perrier. "After all, this is why we call it a château." The notary chuckled.

Amanda walked across the parquet that creaked under her feet. A large canopy bed was placed in the middle of the room. Amanda noticed that the bedframe and the poles were covered with scratches.

"Why is the bed covered with scratches?" she asked.

"Mrs. D'Orvilly had many cats. It was probably too difficult to discipline them, so she let them do whatever they wanted."

It was a shame to see such damaged furniture. But Amanda was amused. Living with crazy cats was something she had in common with Toinette d'Orvilly.

"Where are these cats now?" she asked.

"Some were brought to an animal shelter, and I've been told that one escaped."

Amanda slid a finger along the top of a dusty chest. The windows and the heavy curtains were dirty.

"I apologize for the state of the rooms. Nobody has taken care of this property for a while, and it's been closed for about a year now," said Mr. Perrier. "But all the linens were removed and cleaned just after Mrs. D'Orvilly passed away. They are stored in a closet in the laundry room, downstairs."

Amanda followed the notary to an en suite bathroom. A beautiful claw foot bathtub with golden carved legs was located in the centre. Most of the light green tiles on the floor were cracked, and the old flower wallpaper was peeling off. A stained mirror leaned behind two sinks, and a vanity with a little stool was in a corner. Several flasks of perfume were displayed on the vanity, most of them empty. Amanda imagined Toinette d'Orvilly sitting on the stool, doing her hair in front of the mirror, spraying a cloud of perfume on her neck, getting ready for the day. What did she look like?

"How could Mrs. D'Orvilly live like this?" asked Amanda, "it's an amazing place, but many things are too old, broken, or dilapidated. Did she have financial issues that kept her from maintaining the castle?"

"Hmm... We'll talk about this later if you don't mind," answered the notary.

Odd. Why couldn't he answer this simple question now?

"Let me show you another room," said Mr. Perrier, "a charming lounge. And then we'll go downstairs to see the kitchen."

Amanda followed the man who was holding a little map in his hands. He placed his finger on it, and chose a direction.

"This way..."

He stopped and turned the other way.

"No, pardon me, this way. I apologize, I always get lost in here."

They both walked to the other end of the corridor and went up a spiral staircase.

The corridor on the second floor had the same faded red carpet. Mr. Perrier opened a door on his right that led to a lounge with a wine colored wallpaper, with golden birds on green branches. A few armchairs and coffee tables were placed here and there, and there were books and trifles on dusty shelves. The best feature of the room was a black grand piano placed by the window.

"Did Mrs. D'Orvilly play the piano?" asked Amanda.

"I believe that in her younger years, she did. But I doubt that she ever touched the keyboard of this piano after her husband passed away."

"Did you know her well?"

"I met her on a few occasions for some paperwork related to the estate and her will."

"Was she a nice person?"

"Oh yes, she was a lovely lady. Most people in the village liked her. But frankly, I really didn't know her that well."

"What did she look like?"

Mr. Perrier frowned and looked at the ceiling.

"She was a short lady of petite frame with brown eyes, and white hair that she always kept up in a tight chignon..." The notary pinched his lips. "Hmm, sorry, I realize that I can't think of much more to say about her."

"Are there any pictures or photo albums about the d'Orvilly's kept somewhere?"

"You might find some if you explore the furniture drawers and the closets, or maybe the basement. I'm sorry, but I don't recall finding such things when we did the inventory. But we could've missed them."

A flash of lightening brightened up a wall for a second, revealing several paintings.

"Oh, who's this?"

Amanda pointed to a medium-sized painting. Mr. Perrier got closer to better see it. He squinted, pursing his lips. The painting portrayed a man standing proudly with a dog on his left side, one hand on the dog's head, and the other carrying a black hat under his arm. His sideburns were perfectly trimmed. His long red jacket was open at the front, showing a white shirt underneath. His black boots and black pants looked like one garment. The man had a stern face.

"I have no clue who this man was, sorry Ms. McBride. I guess that there are many things that you have yet to discover about your ancestors... Well, it's getting darker. I'm sorry to shorten the visit, but we can have a quick look at the kitchen now before we go, if you want?"

"Sure," answered Amanda with a grin. If there was one room she wanted to see, it was the kitchen.

They went back to the ground floor and walked down yet another long and narrow corridor.

"Believe it or not," said Mr. Perrier, "despite the narrow width and the long length of this corridor, the kitchen staff used to make hundreds of trips a day to serve their masters. In the old days, I mean."

At the end of the corridor, three stairs led down into a large kitchen. A massive oak counter occupied most of the space in the middle. A large ceramic stove—a gorgeous antique—was placed against the wall that faced them. There were several shelves in a corner on their left, filled with empty jars. Probably the pantry. The only source of light came from a small window above two large porcelain sinks.

Many pans, hung from solid hooks above the working area, attracted Amanda's attention. She felt like a child in a candy store, imagining the fantastic French meals she could cook here.

"Oh my God! All of these are cast-iron pans and pots. And this stove must work with gas, right?"

"Correct," answered Mr. Perrier, "I doubt that you'll find a lot of electrical appliances here, except for the fridge. The electrical circuit is obsolete and dangerous, and this stove should be replaced. I strongly advise you to be cautious if you were to use it."

"Oh, Mr. Perrier, this stove is gorgeous, and there's nothing better than cooking on an old gas stove!"

"If you say so, Ms. McBride. I've never been so much of a cook, to be honest."

"Did Mrs. D'Orvilly like to cook?"

Mr. Perrier chuckled.

"No, Ms. McBride, people like Mrs. D'Orvilly never cooked, and they never did anything by themselves. Mrs. D'Orvilly had servants."

"Really? She had servants? Until she died?"

"Pretty much all her life. But not the last year before she passed away."

"So, what did she eat if she didn't cook and didn't have servants before she died?"

"She ate mostly out of cans. We found a lot of empty tin cans stacked in a bin behind the castle. The odd thing is Mrs. D'Orvilly didn't bother to get rid of them. Cleaning that up wasn't the nicest part of the job when our team did the inventory after her death, if you know what I mean..."

Amanda grimaced. For sure, she and her ancestor didn't share the same interest in canned food. What a shame, she thought, when one owns such an exceptional kitchen worthy of an expert chef.

Mr. Perrier was getting nervous and kept glancing at the corridor. "Sorry to rush you, Ms. McBride, but we should leave now. It will be pitch-black here very soon, and I'd hate to get us lost in this old castle."

The man walked toward the exit and Amanda followed him. As she was about to step out of the kitchen, a sudden flash of lightening lit the room for a fraction of a second, revealing the shape of a person standing in a corner. Amanda yelled.

"What's going on?" asked Mr. Perrier. "Are you all right, Ms. McBride?"

"I just saw someone in the kitchen!"

"You saw someone in the kitchen?"

"Yes, right now!"

"Well, that's odd... Nobody should be here, I'm the only one who has the keys. Are you sure?"

"Yes, over there, in that corner, someone was standing there!"

Mr. Perrier walked back to the kitchen reluctantly, and looked around quickly.

"I'm sorry, but I don't see anybody, Ms. McBride. Maybe what you saw was just the shadow of the pans forming a strange shape on the wall? Don't worry, there's nobody here but us."

Amanda followed the notary who walked hastily to the main door. But as they left the property, she couldn't help but think that what she had seen in the kitchen was without doubt a human shape.

Amanda wasn't the kind to make up stories or see things that weren't there. So, what did she see? Or to be more precise, *who* did she see?

Chapter 16

"Here are the keys and the map, Ms. McBride. I put on stickers to identify them, but with all this rain the writing has faded away. I think the main door key is this one."

Amanda took the heavy ring with the old-style brass keys.

"In a day or two the weather should be better," continued Mr. Perrier. "I suggest that you go back to the castle and take your time to view all the rooms. It will take you a few hours. Please, drop by my office before Friday to inform me about your decision. I have to talk to you about an important matter we haven't had the chance to discuss yet."

"All right Mr. Perrier. Thank you for driving me back."

"You're welcome!"

Amanda closed the door, and the car drove away. She ran to The Little Norman and pushed open the hotel door, relieved to be in a warm place, at last.

She stood in the corridor, soaked from head to toe, water dripping on the floor. Titi ran toward her, barking and showing his teeth.

"Titi, right here, now!"

A short man with a mustache and a crown of grey hair walked toward Amanda, smiling.

"You must be the little Canadian?"

'Little?' Again! Amanda knew she was short, but this odd manner of calling her 'little' was becoming insulting.

"Yes. You must be Mr. Beaudoin?"

"Himself in person! Please, call me Paul."

Paul shook Amanda's hand vigorously.

"You're quite soaked. Did you want to enjoy a shower under the heavy rains of Normandy?" The man showed all his teeth, proud of his joke. Amanda forced a polite smile.

"No, I had to go out to visit a place, and the weather became nasty very quickly. It's so dark outside, and it's only 4 p.m."

"Welcome to Normandy, my dear."

Amanda removed her coat and left her rubber boots at the entrance.

"Wait," said the man, "I'll go and get you a towel."

Paul walked away, but Titi didn't move. He kept staring at Amanda, growling. She bet that the dog would jump up on her immediately if she were to make a single move.

"Here you go," said Paul, handing her a fresh towel.

"Thank you so much."

"What place did you visit? If it's not indiscreet to ask. It must've been really important if you still went despite this bad weather."

"I was the castle," answered Amanda.

"The castle?" Paul looked quite intrigued.

"Yes. The castle. On the Domaine d'Orvilly."

The man frowned and remained silent for a few seconds, as if something were wrong.

"Ah. Yes. This castle," he answered, lowering his tone.

"Are there any other castles in Orvilly?" asked Amanda.

"No. That's the only one."

"So, why do you look surprised?"

The man was hesitant to answer.

"Nothing. Don't worry."

'Don't worry?' What was that supposed to mean? Should she be worried about something?

"If you're hungry," said Paul, "my wife has prepared a good creamy leek soup, and a stew with potatoes. Do you want some? I could prepare you a table quickly in the dining room."

Why did he suddenly change the subject? Amanda was hungry and exhausted. Dining on her own wasn't very appealing, and she was looking forward to seeing d'Artagnan and Bronx.

"I'd love to try your wife's soup and stew, but I'd rather eat in my bedroom, if you don't mind. I'm so tired. Can I take a tray with me upstairs?"

"Of course, you can. Just go up and relax, make yourself warm. I'll bring you a tray in a few minutes."

"Wonderful. Thank you very much, Paul."

Amanda went up the staircase, wondering why Paul had reacted so oddly when she had mentioned the castle. Was there something about this place that Mr. Perrier should've told her? Maybe it was this important matter he wanted to discuss with her?

She would soon find out, but for the moment, she needed two things: eating and resting.

Chapter 17

As soon as Amanda opened the door of her room, d'Artagnan jumped up on her.

Where the hell were you? The dog looked at her as if she had abandoned him for a century. *What did you do all day without me?*

He started to circle around Amanda nervously.

"I know, I know, d'Art. I've been away for a while, sorry. I had something important to do."

She patted the Great Dane's back to calm him down. The dog wagged his tail and stood up on his back legs to put his paws on Amanda's shoulders.

"All right. I promise we'll go out for a walk later."

Someone knocked at the door. Paul entered, carrying a tray, bringing with him divine smells of butter, leeks, beef and brown sauce. D'Artagnan's attention was immediately diverted.

Food! The dog rushed to sniff the tray.

"Oh, oh!" said Paul, "I see that someone here appreciates homemade cuisine."

"Behave, d'Artagnan!" said Amanda.

The dog looked at her. *What? Not doing anything wrong. I'm just sniffing!*

Paul left the tray on the desk. "I added some Camembert and a piece of fresh baguette. And a little glass of red wine, of course." Paul winked. "On the house. Have a good evening, Amanda."

"Thank you very much, Paul."

The man left. D'Artagnan sat beside the desk, keeping his eyes on the dishes. The dog was salivating. *Wow! Is this for us? It smells sooo good!*

Amanda looked for something in the nightstand drawer. D'Artagnan got closer to the tray, slowly, to avoid attracting Amanda's attention.

"Even if my back is turned, d'Art, I know what you're doing. Behave, if you really want a piece of this."

Damn! That's torture, thought the dog.

"Ah. Here it is." Amanda pointed a remote control at the television and pushed a button to turn on the big screen.

"Let's see what's good on French TV, d'Art."

Amanda sat on the bed comfortably and tapped on the mattress. The dog jumped on the bed to lie beside his friend. He put his head three inches away from the tray and stared at the beef stew, in case it tried to escape, you never know.

On the television screen, people sitting in a semi-circle were debating about something. Some of them were speaking quite vehemently. One person was standing up and yelling at another, showing his fist.

"What is this? The French version of The Larry King Show?"

A man in the middle who seemed to be the host show tried to keep control of the situation. It wasn't working, insults were still flying.

"Damn, what are they talking about? It must be important."

Amanda pressed one of the remote control buttons to display on the screen the information about the show. She read out loud. "*'Has French cinema recovered since the New Wave?'*" Amanda looked at d'Artagnan, intrigued. "Wow. I can't believe that they're fighting about that."

The dog mumbled something. *Me neither, and I don't care. Give me this big piece of meat over there. You don't want it, right?*

Amanda took the spoon beside the smoking bowl of soup. Each mouthful of the mellow leek soup titillated Amanda's palate, and so did the tender pieces of Régine's beef stew. The softened Camembert spread on the crusty baguette accompanied perfectly the sips of red wine. Amanda closed her eyes, murmuring her pleasure.

"Now, that's what I call 'fine cuisine,' d'Art."

The dog followed each of Amanda's moves, desperately waiting for her to forfeit her feast.

A few minutes later, a happily sated Amanda fell sound asleep on the bed while the heated debate on the television show kept escalating. People were now literally fighting.

Thrilled that Amanda had 'passed out,' the Great Dane eagerly emptied her plate. *It would be such a shame to let this go to waste!*

The present or the future of French cinema had no relevance to d'Artagnan. All essential things in life were about food. Period.

Chapter 18

The cell phone alarm went off. Amanda awoke with the reminiscence of a dream that was fading away like ripples in a pond.

She was in the castle, feeling lost and scared. It was dark. A woman was running after her, and they switched rooms instantly. Did she want something good or bad? This uncertainty made her feel uneasy.

Amanda heard d'Artagnan barking, but she wasn't sure if it was in her dream or in reality. She opened her eyes and saw the dog standing by the windowsill, his head out of the window.

"Shush d'Artagnan! You'll awake everybody in the hotel and get us in trouble."

Amanda looked around and remembered that she had two companions. One was missing.

"Oh my God. Bronx!"

Amanda ran to the window and stuck her head outside. No cat. She panicked and turned the room upside down, checked under the bed, in the closet, the drawers, the bathtub. Pretty much anywhere an average sized cat could hide. No cat.

D'Artagnan was following her everywhere. *Don't worry, he's gone. It's all good news. No need to make a fuss about it.*

"Oh my God, oh my God, oh my God! Where is he?"

Far away, hoped d'Artagnan.

Amanda put on her bathrobe, slid her feet into her slippers, ran out of the hotel room and slammed the door, leaving d'Artagnan behind.

What? No! Don't leave me alone again!

Amanda hurtled down the stairs and rushed towards the front door. Titi, who was resting on his pillow, saw something passing in front of him as fast as a rocket. Too fast to give him the opportunity to bark. Amanda was already outside, searching frantically for her cat.

"Bronx! Bronx! Where are you?"

All the cars in the streets nearby were clear, no cat was hiding underneath. Amanda ran randomly, taking one street, then another, in hope of finding the fugitive cat. Then, about fifty feet away from her on the sidewalk, she saw an elderly lady leaning over something. The woman was petting an animal, and it was a cat. A cat with black fur on his back, and white fur on his head and paws. No doubt, it was Bronx.

Amanda ran toward the lady, waving her arms in the air.

"Hey! Madam!" yelled Amanda.

When the woman saw a crazy stranger in pajamas running toward her, making threatening moves with her arms, she grabbed the cat, turned around the corner and hurried along the sidewalk as fast as she could. Amanda panicked.

"What? No! Hey! Madam, that is my cat!"

Amanda sped up and turned around the corner, but there was nobody in the street. The lady and the cat had disappeared.

"Where are they?" moaned Amanda.

She walked up the street, carefully looking around. Maybe the lady had gone into a house? Then Amanda stopped abruptly and took a few steps backwards. By the shop window of a bakery, she saw Bronx resting in the arms of the lady who was feeding him little choux buns. The feline was devouring the pastries, giving sweet innocent looks to the lady. It was Bronx in all its glory, putting on another act to get what he wanted.

Amanda put her hands on her hips and frowned. "I can't believe this!" She pushed open the door of the bakery. The smell of fresh bread and pastries should've soothed Amanda's mood, but she was too mad at Bronx for escaping. She pointed an accusing finger at the cat. "You, mister!"

The elderly woman, who was tall and bony, threw a sharp glance at Amanda, and held the cat tight against her chest. Bronx smirked. He was chewing a choux bun like gum, very much enjoying the situation. *This is going to be quite entertaining...* thought the cat.

The woman scanned Amanda with disdain from head to toe. Who was this woman running after her, panting, in a bathrobe and slippers, her hair all messed up? She could only be crazy or homeless.

"What do you want?" asked the woman abruptly.

"I'm glad you found my cat. Thank you."

The lady squinted.

"How do I know it's *your* cat."

"Because I'm telling you."

The elderly woman shrugged.

"It doesn't prove anything. This cat doesn't even have a collar. See. No proof."

Bronx was licking his paws covered with sugar. Amanda could swear the cat was smirking at her.

A man wearing a white apron came from the back store, holding a large plate with warm croissants and pains au chocolat. He displayed the pastries with care on racks behind a glass counter. It was hard not to notice him. Tall, well built, with dark hair and blue eyes. Probably in his forties, and the most important detail, incredibly handsome.

"What's going on?" he asked the women, with a smile.

"Hello," said Amanda, "I'm trying to explain to this lady that this is my cat."

Amanda pointed at Bronx. The woman turned her head to the baker.

"Who knows if this is really hers?" she said, with a defensive tone. Then she leaned to the counter. "I think she's insane," she whispered. "Look at her."

The man looked at Amanda and smiled again. Amanda blushed.

"Mrs. Parmentier, if this lady says it's her cat, I believe her. I've never seen this cat around here before, and I know for sure that he's not your cat, right?"

The woman turned her head and let out an offended 'pfff!'

"I'm not lying. This is my cat," said Amanda. "I'm staying at the hotel over there, The Little Norman. You can call them and ask them if you want."

"No need to do that," said the dreamy baker, "Mrs. Parmentier will give you back your cat because she *can't* take him with her in her senior home anyway. Right, Germaine?"

The man gave a pointed look at the woman. Mrs. Parmentier exhaled another 'pfff' and handed the cat to Amanda, reluctantly. Bronx emitted a weak 'meow.' The cat was falling asleep, feeling the effects of the sugar overdose he had swallowed.

"Thank you," said Amanda.

"Hmm," grunted Mrs. Parmentier.

In a quick move, Mrs. Parmentier grabbed a bag full of pastries from the counter, and left, giving Amanda a last cold look before she closed the door.

"I'm so sorry, sir," said Amanda. "I feel terrible, and I know all this looks odd, but—"

"No worries," replied the man, "no need to explain yourself. What's the name of your cat?"

"Bronx."

"Bronx?" The sexy baker laughed. "He must be a rough cat to have earned such a tough name."

"He is indeed. He escaped from the hotel room, and I was scared that something bad might happen to him. He's used to doing things like this just to make me crazy. But I love him. I've had him since he was a kitten."

"Are you here visiting? You have an accent. Are you American?"

"No, I'm Canadian. I'm not sure yet if I'm just visiting or staying."

The baker took a white paper bag, put a few croissants in it, and handed it to Amanda with a warm smile. "Here's to welcome you, hoping that you'll stay."

Amanda blushed again and melted inside. She wanted to hide under a counter, and wished she had listened to her friend Kate, for once. She looked like a grungy wacko in front of, well, the most attractive man she had seen for a long time. And he was French. Moreover, a baker.

"Oh, you don't have to... I have money," she said.

The man laughed. "I know. It's my pleasure to offer you these. I'm Pierre, by the way."

The man presented his hand, waiting for a handshake. Amanda shook his hand.

"I'm Amanda."

"Pleased to meet you, Amanda." She walked to the door, feeling a bit disoriented, and hit her head first on the glass. Pierre laughed.

"You have to open the door. This is how it works," said the baker.

"Yes, I know..." stammered Amanda. Could she embarrass herself more?

Amanda walked back to the hotel with Bronx sleeping and snoring in her arms. The cat had been lucky to end his spree in a bakery, his greedy stomach fed with pastries.

A grin grew on Amanda's face. She caressed the cat and whispered, "Bronx, right now I don't know if I should ground you or if I should thank you."

Chapter 19

"Jeez, thish guy ish increjibly hanshome!"

"What?" asked Kate.

Amanda swallowed the big chunk of croissant she was chewing.

"This guy is incredibly handsome."

"Hmm... A French hot guy, moreover a baker," said Kate, reveling in the exciting news, "I like that. It sounds promising. For once, Bronx did something good. So, how did the visit at the castle go?"

Amanda was lying on the bed, talking on the phone with her friend, while d'Artagnan lay at her feet, eating a couple of croissants directly from the paper bag. Bronx was sleeping on a chair, snoring. The cat was resting on his back in an odd position, his legs straight up in the air.

"To be honest, I don't know what to think about the castle," answered Amanda. "The visit was pretty scary."

"Scary? What do you mean?"

"First, this property is huge. I mean, really *huge*. A castle is way too big for me."

"Come on, that's exciting! You love old castles, antiques, and anything labeled as 'French.'"

"Yes, but yesterday I wasn't so much into it. It was pouring like hell—not much of a change from rain in Victoria, you will you me, but it was even worse than what we're used to—and it was very dark. And there were thunder rumbling, lightning... the place was spooky. I even saw something weird in the kitchen."

"What? A ghost?" said Kate with a teasing tone.

"Very funny, Kate. But I'm serious. Just as lightning brightened up the kitchen for a second, I saw the shape of someone in a corner as we were leaving the room. Mr. Perrier checked the room, but saw nobody. But I swear I saw someone standing there."

"It must've been your imagination mixed with all the stress and the bad weather, don't worry about that. So, how many rooms does this castle have?"

"Twenty-four! And when I say twenty-four, you can double the number easily to have a better idea of the area. These rooms are gigantic and at least as twice large as our regular rooms. Can you imagine doing the housework in this place? It must be hell. I can't do this, I'm telling you. That's the problem, it's way too big. What would I do with an old castle with twenty-four rooms? It must cost a fortune to maintain it. Plus, it needs serious repairs, and I don't have the money for this. Honestly, Kate, I think that I should just give it up and go to the south of France now as I had planned."

"Wait until your second visit before making any decision, and talk about this with Mr. Perrier. Maybe there are solutions that would help you keep the castle?"

"Like what? Winning the lottery? I never play."

"I don't know... something like grants for the restoration and preservation of heritage buildings?"

"Maybe... but I can't count on that, it's way too risky. I don't feel good about all this, Kate. Sure, it's France, and it's fun, but I have to be realistic: maybe this inheritance is more a pain in the ass than the romantic French life I had imagined."

"Don't give up now, Amanda. You just arrived in Orvilly, and you haven't even seen the full castle yet. Visit it again, and take the time you need to make a sound decision. I understand why all this can be scary, but don't rush things, if not you might regret making the wrong decision the rest of your life."

"The problem is that I have to give an answer to the notary by the end of this week. It doesn't leave me much time to reflect on such an important matter that will impact the rest of my life."

"Don't bite your sister! Don't you—"

Amanda frowned. This last advice was probably not for her. She heard children shouting and crying on the other end of the phone.

"Sorry, but I have to go," said Kate, "Joshua recently discovered that he could bite people, especially his sister. I have to end this game before my terrifying two-year-old eats his older sister alive. Talk to you later!"

D'Artagnan was still chewing the fresh croissants. The bag of viennoiseries was empty.

"Thanks for sharing, d'Art."

No problem, smiled d'Artagnan, with pieces of croissant were stuck between his teeth.

Chapter 20

Three quick honks, sharp and hoarse, as if the car had caught a bad cold. It was the signal.

Amanda put her head out of the window to look down on Brigadier Street. Liliane, the woman she had met in the train, was waiting in an old Citroën 2CV—a 'Deux Chevaux' or a 'Deudeuche,' as the French call it fondly—parked in front of the hotel. Liliane thrust her arm out the driver's window and waved at Amanda who waved back. Then Amanda rushed to put on her running shoes and then grabbed her raincoat. The weather looked agreeable in Orvilly-sur-Mer, but after the rains she had experienced the previous day, she already knew better than to leave her room without protection.

She took d'Artagnan's leash from the doorknob. The Great Dane jumped all over the place.

I'm going out! I'm going out! I'm going out!

Bronx was on the windowsill. The cat raised his eyes to the ceiling, sighing with exasperation. *Yes, you're going out, dumb dog! And do me a favor, don't ever come back.*

Amanda locked the three windows carefully and stroked Bronx's head. The feline frowned.

Crap. No escape to the bakery today.

"Be a good cat, Bronx. We'll see you later."

And within a few seconds, Amanda and d'Artagnan were on the sidewalk, ready to go for a sightseeing tour of Orvilly-sur-Mer and the surrounding area. Liliane had kindly offered to be their guide for the day.

When Amanda opened the back passenger door and asked d'Artagnan to get in, the dog looked at her with round eyes.

Are you kidding? It's smaller than my sofa at home! I'm never going to fit in! Why is everything so tiny here?

After a few strategic moves that required gymnastic contortions, the Great Dane finally took his place in the back seat. But he couldn't move an inch.

When Amanda went to open the front passenger door, she stopped and stared at the door, intrigued. Strangely enough, she couldn't find a handle. There was none. Liliane laughed when she saw Amanda's face.

"This is an old model made in the fifties, so the handle is on the other side." She pointed with her finger toward the front of the car.

Amanda found the small handle, that could easily be missed, and pushed it down to open the door backwards. It felt strange and quite impractical to step into the vintage car this way.

"Who came up with this twisted idea?" asked Amanda.

"I don't know," said Liliane. "But when I tell you what we call these doors, I'm not sure you'll want to touch them ever again."

Amanda was afraid to ask. But she did.

"They're called 'suicide doors,'" said Liliane.

Amanda turned pale. "What?"

Liliane laughed even more when she saw the panic on Amanda's face.

"I'm not sure if I should ask why..." said Amanda.

"But I'll tell you anyway. Citroën, the company that started to build this car at the end of the forties, quickly realized that these doors were dangerous because they would suddenly open and tear off, causing accidents, and leaving the drivers and the passengers without protection. So they were given the name 'suicide doors.' After the sixties, however, this model was built with regular doors."

Amanda was speechless. Liliane grinned, still amused by Amanda's reaction, and started the car. The vehicle trumpeted and trembled, then stalled. Amanda gave an anxious sideways look to Liliane, strongly doubting that any sightseeing tour would be possible. Liliane replied with a simple smile. Not worried the least, the woman tried to start the car again. It trumpeted and trembled again for a few seconds, then settled down to a regular vibration, and then they took off slowly.

"So, tell me, Liliane, why do you have an old dangerous car? Are you suicidal?"

Liliane laughed. "Of course not. But this old car is so much fun to drive! It belonged to my father who loved it. I kept it went he passed away, and I love taking care of it. This is a collector's car, you know."

The light green Deudeuche moved forward on Brigadier Street, making a rattling noise like nails tumbling in a dryer, expelling black clouds through the exhaust pipe. The few pedestrians on the sidewalks didn't seem to be bothered by it and kept walking as if everything were normal. But Amanda had serious doubts the crumbling Citroën would get them very far. She realized that she liked antiques, but not being driven in them.

Sitting by one of the windows of the hotel room, Bronx meowed as he watched the car driving off. He was ecstatic. *Ha ha! Good luck with that old junker!*

❀

D'Artagnan's long ears were flying in the wind. Head out of the window and mouth wide open, the dog was enjoying the fresh air of Normandy, tickled by the gusts flapping his skin. He was counting the cows in the green fields of the countryside.

52, 53, 54… Damn! It never ends! There are more cows than people here.

"You inherited the castle? You're the heiress? That's unbelievable!" said Liliane.

"Yes, well, I haven't signed any papers yet," said Amanda. "I have to make a decision by the end of this week though, and I really don't know what to do. It must be costly to maintain such a big property, and I don't have that kind of money. Honestly, I'm not sure if I'd be able to live there. Toinette d'Orvilly must've felt so lonely in this big castle. Did you ever meet her?"

"Yes, on a few occasions when she was shopping in the village. She was always very agreeable and polite, but she wouldn't engage much with them. We barely saw her the year before she passed away though. It seemed that she had decided to live in seclusion."

"Do you know why?"

"Not really. She was quite old, in her nineties, I believe, and she had no family left. So, maybe she felt more comfortable staying in the castle in the company of her cats? Who knows. I heard she had quite a few. I also know that she was fed up being bothered by undesirable visitors on her property."

"What do you mean?"

"You know, tourists and nosy people. Some of them were passionate about medieval castles and kept coming onto the property, although it's clearly marked private, sometimes knocking at her door, asking to tour the castle, which she didn't want to do. Teenagers tried to break in at night, and some potential buyers offered her millions of Euros for the estate. But she didn't want to sell. She had lived in the castle all her life, so it was her home. What would she have done with millions of Euros anyway, with no family, knowing well that she was reaching the end of her life? She always refused to sell it. She really loved this castle."

Liliane turned to the left and passed through a gate to drive onto a path running through a field. A sign, with a smiling red apple drawn on it, read 'Morin's Pommeraie and Cider House.'

"Do you like apple cider, Amanda? I promise you Morin has the best in the area."

The wheels of the Deux Chevaux crunched on the gravel when Liliane parked the car in front of the farm. She stopped the vehicle abruptly, flinging its passengers forward. The car made a clunky noise. Liliane pulled the white, golf-balled sized knob of the hand break towards herself. The long metal rod, built into the dashboard, produced an unpleasant grinding noise as she pulled it.

Amanda stepped out of the car carefully, unsure yet how to manipulate the strange reverse door. Once out, she opened the door to the back seat. D'Artagnan jumped out of the car, happy to escape and stretch his legs. Amanda felt the same way. All along the bumpy ride in the old car, their behinds had jiggled on the metal structure underneath the thin cushions. Liliane was all smiles, obviously used to this, probably thinking it was part of the charm of driving an old Deudeuche.

All three walked to the entrance of the farmhouse, where several barrels filled with red apples were displayed. D'Artagnan sniffed a few.

Can I—

"Nope! You can't, d'Art," immediately said Amanda, giving her dog a stern look.

Damn! That's torture! Frustrated, the Great Dane mumbled and walked into the building.

"Welcome to Morin's Pommeraie and Cider House," said a young woman with an inviting smile. She was placing bottles of cider on shelves. "Is this your first visit here?"

"Not for me," answered Liliane, "but it is for my friend."

The young woman left her bottles and walked with enthusiasm toward Amanda.

"All right then. My name is Florine and it will be a pleasure to tell you our story. The Pommeraie and Cider House was founded in 1918 by Ernest Morin." The young woman pointed at framed black and white pictures hung on a wall. "Ernest was a young soldier at that time, only 17, when he came home to the family farm after fighting on the front lines during World War I. Unfortunately, upon his return, he mostly found ruins. The main building of the farm had been severely damaged. But the worst part was learning that he had lost his entire family. Nobody had survived the war. The young man showed a lot of courage and, with the help of a few villagers, rebuilt the family farm and took care of the orchard where his parents had once grown apple trees. Ernest worked hard, took care of the existing trees, and planted new ones. Soon, he was able to make a decent living selling apples. When his business flourished, he decided to start producing cider. The quality of his cider made Ernest's business popular very quickly, and Morin Cider gained its reputation as an excellent cider, and even one of the best in the region. In 1922, Ernest married a young woman from the village, Marie Dupuis, and started his own family. Today, it is one of his great-grand-daughters, Claire, who runs the family business, who happens to be my mother. We're proud to say that our sweet Morin Cider has won the Golden Medal for Best Cider in Normandy three years in a row. Would you like to taste a sample?"

"After such a wonderful story, how can I say no?" answered Amanda.

"And you madam, would you like one too?" asked the young woman, turning to Liliane.

"Sure. Just a tiny sample though. I'm the one driving."

Florine went behind the counter and opened a bottle. She poured cider into two small glasses and handed them to Amanda and Liliane. As the two friends were sipping their drinks, a rotating stand beside them attracted Amanda's attention. She turned the stand to look through the postcards with pictures of cliffs and pebble beaches that made Normandy so famous, old farmhouses made of white cob and beams, and people in horse-drawn carriages rolling along the paved streets of quaint Orvilly-sur-Mer in the early twentieth century.

A black and white postcard piqued her curiosity. Amanda recognized the castle, in front of which posed a group of people beside a black luxury car. The men were dressed elegantly in black suits with long jackets, and the women wore evening dresses. A young woman in the center of the group wore a white gown with a long veil, and held a bouquet. Amanda took the postcard and turned it to read the inscription on the back. She read *'Wedding of Toinette d'Orvilly and Abélard de Marsan, Orvilly-sur-Mer, June 1948.'*

Amanda's face brightened. "Look, Liliane! This is a picture of Toinette d'Orvilly in 1948. This is the first picture I've seen of her."

Liliane took the postcard and smiled.

"She is so young in this picture. Probably in her mid-twenties at that time? Her gown is lovely. I remember that she loved fashion and was always polished and chic, even in her older years. I believe Abélard de Marsan was her first husband who died only two years after the wedding in a car accident. Very sad. She was too young to become a widow." Liliane looked at Amanda and squinted. "You know what? I think you look a bit like her."

"Me?" said Amanda, doubtful. She took back the postcard and scrutinized it. Did she really look like Toinette? Maybe. Maybe they had some features in common, as well as their love of animals. Obviously, she and her ancestor didn't share the same love for fashion though. But could they share the same love for the castle?

Chapter 21

At last, a blue sky with only a few clouds. Rays of sunshine warmed up Orvilly-sur-Mer, giving the village this Norman charm Amanda had seen in pictures of Normandy.

"Get ready d'Art, we're going for a walk someplace special."

Amanda was waving the dog's leash and d'Artagnan was jumping in the room, making it difficult for her to clip the strap on his collar.

"Please, d'Art, stop moving so that I can clip the leash on your collar, if you want to get out of here."

The dog calmed down.

"There you go. It wasn't that hard, was it?"

Bronx was sleeping on the windowsill, snoring loudly as usual, moving his paws as if he were fighting. Amanda checked on him to make sure the cat was all right.

D'Artagnan moved his tail impatiently. *Focus on me, not him. We were about to leave, remember?*

"All right, let's go d'Art."

The dog pulled so hard on his leash that Amanda had to hold on tight to the rail to avoid falling down the stairs.

"Slow down, d'Art!"

They arrived downstairs quickly, and in one piece. Mrs. Beaudoin was behind the counter, absorbed in reading a magazine.

"Good morning, Régine."

"'Boujou," answered Régine. The woman just waved a hand and barely lifted her head.

Amanda and d'Artagnan were stopped at the front door, a terrible threat blocking their way. Titi was posted there, growling and showing his teeth. The tiny dog was on a mission: nobody would pass that door.

D'Artagnan looked down on the dog. *This is a joke, right? Move away before I eat you, ugly rat.*

Titi barked.

"Uh, Régine, we have a little problem..." said Amanda.

"Titi, come here!" yelled Régine, her nose still in her magazine.

But the little dog ignored the woman's order and didn't move one inch. He was bouncing on his front legs, as if he were ready to attack.

D'Artagnan was getting impatient. *Can I eat him now?*

A hand grabbed Titi and lifted the dog into the air. "You, mister, how many times have I told you not to scare our guests? You're just the size of a little shrimp." Régine put the dog back on his pillow. "Now, don't you move, Titi," ordered Régine, pointing an authoritarian finger at the tiny dog.

"Sorry about that," said Régine, "this dog thinks that he's as big as yours and he has the same anger issues as the Hulk. Don't you?" said Régine, patting Titi's green rooster comb. The little dog growled.

"Will you have lunch here?" asked Régine to Amanda. "We have very few guests at this time of year, and I'd like to know if I should prepare a table for you or not."

"Oh no, don't worry about me, Régine. I'll probably eat out for lunch, but I'll eat here for supper."

"All right, see you later then."

Amanda and d'Artagnan started their stroll on Brigadier Street.

"We have about a thirty-minute walk, d'Art. Good enough to stretch your legs."

The dog wagged his tail. *Cool! Where are we going?*

Amanda walked on the paved road to let d'Artagnan walk on the narrow sidewalk. Most of the old houses still had typical Normandy windows divided into squares, with wooden shutters. The flowerpots hung on the windowsills added some cheerful spots of color to the white and brown walls. Very few people were walking in the street. The village was still quiet at the beginning of April, with few visitors. But when May came, tourists from France and from all over the world invaded the little historical place.

Amanda and d'Artagnan passed by a lovely shop painted with pastel colors of lilac and green. A cup of tea and little cakes were drawn on the sign above the storefront that read *The Secrets*. Smelling sugar, the Great Dane stopped at once.

"What a cute little shop," said Amanda. "We might stop by later to buy something. Come on d'Art."

But d'Artagnan didn't move. The dog was mesmerized by a gorgeous strawberry cake behind the glass window of the storefront. *Why later? We're here now. Sounds perfect to me.*

In the shop, four elderly ladies sat at a table were enjoying tea and pastries, engaging in what seemed to be a lively conversation. One of them turned her head to look at the storefront and pointed an accusing finger at Amanda. Amanda recognized Mrs. Parmentier, the unpleasant lady she had met in the bakery. The other ladies turned their heads too and stared at Amanda, frowning and shaking their heads with disapproval.

"Oh my!" said Amanda. "It seems that I'm identified as an enemy, now. Come quick before I get in trouble, d'Art."

Not convinced by this argument, the dog sat down and swept his eyes a few times from Amanda to the cake, and from the cake to Amanda.

"I have a surprise for you," declared Amanda with a smile, hoping that this trick would work. The word 'surprise' made it for the dog who stood up immediately. *A surprise! What is it? Can you eat it?*

Amanda quickly walked d'Art away from the shop. When they arrived at the Domaine d'Orvilly, Amanda stood below the iron arch, looking at the castle with amazement. "Wow. It looks so different now," she whispered.

The ivy on the facade gave a romantic allure to the castle. It covered part of the frontispiece over the main door where the coat of arms of the d'Orvilly's was carved into the stone. The tall windows didn't look terrifying anymore, but rather elegant, and the towers at the extremities of the old building seemed to stand proudly as if glad to welcome visitors.

Amanda imagined Toinette d'Orvilly standing beside her, looking at the castle. She felt un unexpected sense of pride rising in her. Maybe she belonged here, after all? She smiled. How amazing to think that she was the descendant of a prestigious French family with such a rich history.

She unleashed d'Artagnan who bounded free like a happy fool on the vast property while she ambled slowly on the path that lead to the front door. Chestnut trees bordered the lane, and apple trees had already started to blossom, revealing their delicate white flowers. Some of these trees had probably witnessed the history of the d'Orvilly's through the centuries.

Amanda walked up the stairs leading to the entrance door and pulled the heavy key holder from her bag. "Which one was it? Mr. Perrier said this one... No, this one... Damn. Which one is it?"

All the keys looked alike. Amanda had no other choice but to try one key after another. After a few unsuccessful attempts, she heard the click she was hoping for, and the heavy door unlocked. She pushed it and called d'Artagnan. The dog ran toward her, and they entered the hall together.

D'Artagnan inspected the place right away, running his muzzle all over the tile floor. He circled around the hall for a few times, going along the four archways that led to different parts of the castle. *Gee, it's a bit coldish in here, isn't it? Is there food somewhere?*

"How come I missed that the other day?"

Amanda stood in front of a big painting hung on the wall that faced the entrance door. It was placed above a large fireplace.

The artwork in a gilded frame depicted an elegant young woman, probably in her twenties, who stood by an Empire armchair. She wore a voluminous white evening gown, the short sleeves fell off her delicate shoulders, and a pearl necklace embellished her décolleté. One of her hands rested on the top of the armchair. Amanda noticed a golden bracelet around her wrist. A funny little dog with long ears sat proudly at the young woman's feet. His white and brown fur looked pristine, probably groomed to perfection that day for the occasion. An inscription etched in a little golden plate at the bottom of the frame: 'Duchesse Mélie D'Orvilly, 1862.'

"Well, d'Art, I think that I just met one of my ancestors. Isn't she beautiful?"

Not paying the least attention to the painting, the Great Dane decided to keep exploring the new place on his own and ran away in a corridor.

"D'Art, wait! Stay here! We're going to get lost!" Amanda ran after the dog and followed him until they arrived in a vast room. "Stop d'Art! You're going too fast for me!"

The dog obeyed, finally, and paused to give his friend some respite. *Why am I the one who always must slow down? It's not fun. Run faster or grow longer legs.*

The dark cherry scratched parquet had a lozenge pattern. Four high windows on one side let in rays of sunshine that brightened up the room. The walls were covered with a dark brown fabric embroidered with tree branches made of yellow-golden thread. Amanda's steps echoed as she walked in the vast room. She lifted her head and saw three majestic chandeliers with beads of crystal hanging from the ceiling.

"Oh my... this must've been a grandiose ballroom."

D'Artagnan put his head in one of the two fireplaces placed at each end of the room.

"Don't do this d'Art! It's dirty."

The dog sneezed a cloud of black dust and escaped again, passing through a large open doorway, and turned to his left. He stopped when he faced a narrow wooden staircase. Usually, the dog would've turned around, but today his curiosity was stronger than his dislike for stairs. The Great Dane climbed them the best he could, his paws sliding on the steps, and his butt swinging as he moved up.

"Not so fast, d'Art... Oh! Look at this lovely library."

High shelves running from the floor to the ceiling covered the walls of the little room. They were filled with old books. Amanda picked up a dusty book, but she had barely opened it before d'Artagnan was again on the run.

Amanda sighed. At least, at this pace, they'd finish their visit soon. She kept following d'Artagnan.

❖

After two hours of running from one room to another, Amanda sat on the floor of a bedroom. She was panting.

"D'Art. I need a break. Please."

The dog stopped and sat in front of her. *Fine. I give you one minute, that's it.*

She passed her finger over the map of the castle that she was holding in her hands.

"I think we went through most of the rooms. You know what, d'Art? I imagined that living in a castle would be more relaxing than that, but I realize now that I'd need a cart to go from one room to another."

While catching her breath, Amanda noticed a doll house in a corner, near a twin bed. She got up and walked toward it. As she got closer, she realized that it was a perfect replica of the castle. She kneeled in front of it and tried to open it to see inside, but it was locked on the side. A small key was required to open it. "One thing is sure, d'Art, I don't have such a small key on my key holder. I would've noticed it." She looked through the windows, amused to discover the little rooms furnished with miniature pieces. Was it from the 19th century? Amanda pushed her finger through a window, trying to grab the figurine of a lady in a white dress, when she heard something rolling on the floor behind her. D'Artagnan barked. She was startled and stood up to look around her.

"Hello? Is there anybody here?"

Below a stool placed by the bed, a porcelain teacup rolled on the floor. Amanda picked it up. The chipped cup had pink and purple flowers painted on it, and traces of scratched letters written in gold on one side. Amanda could only guess that one of them was an 'O,' probably for Orvilly. She glanced around the room, looking for the rest of the porcelain tea set, but didn't see anything. "What is this cup doing here?" she whispered.

Maybe she could find the rest of the set in the kitchen? But her last visit there had not been the most pleasant one. Amanda called d'Artagnan who still intrigued by the doll house. The dog walked toward her and sat in front of her, showing his sudden docility. *Is it the moment? Are you going to give me my surprise now?*

"D'Artagnan, now's the time to show me that you do love me, and not only because I feed you. You must show me that you can protect me too. We're going to the kitchen."

Did you say 'kitchen?' I'm all for it!

Amanda slowly went down the steps that lead to the kitchen, but stopped at the last one. D'Artagnan pushed her to the side with his head and came straight into the room, sniffing every corner with great enthusiasm. Even if this kitchen hadn't been used for a long time, the dog could still smell food. He looked at Amanda who was still standing on the last step, hesitant, wondering why she had suddenly become scared of kitchens. *Step in! It's just a kitchen. What's wrong with you?*

Finally, Amanda went down the last step. She opened a large cupboard on her left where she found pans, pots, utensils, and several dinnerware sets, but no porcelain tea set.

She turned around and saw a closed door in the far back of a corner. The corner where she had seen the human shape standing. She felt chills running all over her skin and stared at the door for a few seconds. It was locked with a big chain. Should she unlock this door or not? Mustering up her courage and trusting that her dog would defend her if something were to happen, Amanda grabbed the key ring in her bag and tried all the keys in the lock. None of them worked. In a way, she felt relieved. "That's odd. Mr. Perrier must've forgotten to give me the key to this lock. Anyway, let's go, d'Art."

The dog, who was licking a paper, raised his head. He was dumbfounded. *What do you mean 'let's go?' Where's my surprise?*

Amanda looked by the window above the porcelain sinks. "Awesome! Let's go outside, d'Art!" Amanda left the teacup on the counter and ran outside.

D'Artagnan followed her slowly, mumbling. *Ah, now you're running! I have the unpleasant feeling that someone tricked me...*

Amanda and d'Artagnan walked through an abandoned garden located behind the castle, guarded by a stone fence. Weeds had encroached on the garden, and old tables and chairs were covered by ivy and brambles, giving a nostalgic imprint of the past.

"Be careful where you put your nose, d'Art, you could hurt yourself."

My nose? I walk with my paws!

They walked cautiously, striding over many obstacles. Then d'Artagnan stopped. The dog was reluctant to go in any direction, none of them looked like a viable option for him. *Why did you bring us here?*

"D'Art, can you hear that?"

Hear what? The dog was sniffing with mistrust something on the ground.

"Waves! It's waves!" Amanda ran toward the other end of the garden and found a way out that lead to a rusty gate. She forced it open.

D'Artagnan was still behind, trying to get rid of weeds that had curled around one of his paws. *Not so fast! I'm going to break my delicate legs!*

The gate gave away. The two friends left the garden and arrived at a cliff with a breathtaking view of the ocean. A few boats were sailing offshore. They could hear gulls shouting and waves breaking on the rocks.

"Well, now that's a view."

D'Artagnan walked cautiously toward the edge of the cliff.

"Stop now, d'Art!"

The dog startled. *Damn! You want to give me a heart attack or what?*

"It's dangerous."

You think?! Humans, sometimes...

Amanda turned around to admire the landscape and the castle under the sun of Normandy. She smiled and closed her eyes to let herself daydream for a few seconds. A knight was riding a horse, galloping toward her, like in those old cloak and dagger French movies she had watched many times. The steed stopped by Amanda, and the knight offered his hand, inviting her to join him. She raised her head. Blinded by the sun, she shielded her eyes with her hands and saw a handsome man looking exactly like... Pierre? Yes. It was Pierre, the baker. She opened her eyes. "Hmm. Interesting…"

The dreamy appearance of Pierre naturally brought images of pastries and little breads in Amanda's mind. Her stomach growled. "Well, I think it's time we go and eat something, d'Art."

Ah! Finally. I thought you'd never get to that because I'm STARVING!

Chapter 22

Amanda sat at a table beside the large window to better see the activity in the circular marketplace with its old fountain in the middle. Although not as busy as a city center, it was the 'core' of Orvilly-sur-Mer where people came and went, took a stroll, or met for a chat. It was also a gathering point for tourists in summer who needed to refresh themselves and rest for a while. Two old men wearing black berets were sitting on a bench in front of the fountain, one of them waving his cane in the air as he was speaking to his friend.

The Old Calvados was the only bistro in the village that also sold tobacco and lottery games, and so was usually busy. The place was filled with locals eating a quick lunch before heading back to work. A group of men drinking wine and beer were standing by the counter or sitting on high stools, having lively discussions.

Roger Poutou, the owner of the bistro, had allowed Amanda to come inside with d'Artagnan. Upon their arrival, his old Bassett Hound, Georgina, had progressed very slowly in direction to Amanda's table, her heavy and low belly sweeping the floor. She had in mind to welcome d'Artagnan who was sitting quietly by Amanda's feet. The Great Dane was staring at her, intrigued. He had never seen a dog without legs. Did she have legs? Anyway, they'd probably be done with their meals by the time she'd reach their table.

Amanda perused the menu. The selection was not extensive, but she felt inspired by a salade cauchoise and ordered a piece of raw steak for d'Artagnan. Roger returned quickly with a little basket containing slices of baguette and a plate generously piled with potato salad. D'Artagnan pounced on his bowl of fresh meat.

"Anything else for you, madam?" asked Roger.

"No, thank you," answered Amanda.

The tall man smiled, wished her a 'bon appétit' and walked back behind the counter to resume the discussion with the men.

As she ate, Amanda reviewed the pros and cons of owning a castle, considering the possibility of moving into the château, and turning it into a fancy Inn—and maybe even opening her own restaurant?

Kate would be euphoric about this—Amanda's curiosity piqued when she heard the words 'old castle.'

"They're going to tear it down, I tell you," said a man standing at the bar.

"Nah! They still haven't found the heir," said another. "They must find the heir first. They can't do anything if they don't find the new owner."

"Not true," pursued a third man, "if they can't find them, it could become public property."

"And what would the Government do with it? A museum?"

"Not necessarily. They could very well leave it like this and let it fall into pieces, slowly. It's way too expensive to take care of these castles nowadays. Even the French nobility doesn't want them anymore. It's like throwing money into a sinkhole. They prefer to get rid of them. Some even sell them for a single Euro."

"Even for a Euro, I wouldn't buy those old ruins. And I don't want to live with ghosts, thanks."

A few men laughed.

"Again, that old story! Old ladies' gossip, that's all they are."

A man frowned.

"Not true. I know guys who've seen things."

"Yeah! Me too, I know a bunch of guys who've seen a bunch of weird things, especially after having a few drinks!"

The group of men laughed out loud, except for one.

"I know what I'm saying. It's not gossip."

"So, tell me, Gérald, have you ever seen a ghost there?"

Gérald remained silent for a few seconds.

"No. I haven't seen any ghosts," he answered with a small voice, "but some people have!"

The group of men laughed again, making fun of Gérald, patting him on the back. Gérald looked at the floor sourly.

"I know what I'm saying," insisted Gérald, as if he had to defend himself.

Amanda was eating her potatoes, thinking they might have been a tiny overcooked. She looked at d'Artagnan. "Well, d'Art, it seems that we need to have a serious discussion with Mr. Perrier. Obviously, there's something important he's hidden from us."

Fine. But let's do this after I'm done with my steak.

While d'Artagnan was gobbling his last piece of meat, Georgina was halfway across the room. And still walking.

"I can assure you, Ms. McBride, that these are merely old rumors and silly stories," said Mr. Perrier, pushing his glasses up on his nose for the third time.

"Even Paul Beaudoin, the owner of The Little Norman, reacted oddly when I mentioned the castle to him," said Amanda.

Mr. Perrier joined his hands in front of him. "Amanda—may I call you Amanda?"

She nodded in approval.

"Amanda, you have to understand that we're in a small village where gossip, fables, and myths are discussed all the time. People are bored so they need to make up stories to entertain themselves. That's all."

"Well, at least, I want to know what the stories are."

"I really don't think that this 'folklore' is relevant or helpful in this case. They are in no way official information related to the file."

"It's relevant to me because I might decide to become the owner of this castle. But I need to know *everything* you know about it before I make my decision. So, what do people say about it?"

Amanda was staring at the notary with a very determined look. Mr. Perrier nervously adjusted his position in his seat.

"Fine. Some people say that they've been chased at night by a ghost threatening them with a frying pan, which—if you want my opinion—might've just been Toinette d'Orvilly herself running after undesirable visitors on her property, as sometimes happened. Teenagers like to come at night around the castle, seeking 'ghosts.' They see what they want to see, helped by what they drink or smoke, mostly to tell spooky stories to their friends afterward."

"What else?"

The notary sighed. "Others who have been in the castle to do some repairs reported seeing doors closing or opening for no reason. But this is a medieval castle, an uneven floor or a little wind can easily do that."

"Is there more?"

Mr. Perrier hesitated for a moment. He rubbed his hands nervously. "Hmm… All right, this one might frighten you, but you shouldn't be afraid." Still, the man looked a bit anxious.

Amanda leaned toward the desk. What was he about to tell her? "I'm all ears," she said.

"Once, a man delivered some boxes and put them in the basement, at Mrs. D'Orvilly's request. He had a heart attack there. And died at the hospital later that day."

"That's horrible. What happened in the basement?" asked Amanda, not so sure that she wanted to know the answer.

"Well, this is the problem. This man was alone, so nobody saw what happened."

"Was he able to say anything before he died?"

"Only his wife was with him when he passed away. But since then, she passed away too. Hard to know the truth. And it was a long time ago. We're talking about a story that's twenty years old. Again, people who keep talking about this just keep embellishing it and making it worse. I've been told that this man was close to retirement at that time, and might've had health issues that triggered the heart attack."

"So, what do people say about this story, Mr. Perrier?"

The notary sighed again. "Some people say that something 'evil' locked the door while the poor man was alone in the basement and that he was yelling 'go away!' while trying to escape. They had to break the lock on the door to open it, and found the poor man unconscious on the floor."

The basement. That's the only place Amanda couldn't access when she visited the castle.

"Mr. Perrier, do you have the key to the basement?" asked Amanda.

Mr. Perrier looked surprised. "I reckon that I gave you all the keys. You don't have it? "

"No, this one is missing. And it is the only one missing."

"Hmm..." The notary remained pensive for a few seconds. "That's odd. It must've been mislaid... I'll look into this and will give you the key as soon as we find it." The man opened a file on his desk. "Anyway. Amanda, I told you earlier this week that there was something important that I needed to discuss with you." The notary's face lit up. He smiled. "Something much better and more important than these silly ghost stories. Well, you see, even if your great-great-cousin didn't take care of the castle, it isn't because she lacked the finances to do it. As I mentioned before, the death of her second husband affected her deeply. She just didn't care anymore about anything in general, but she did love her family castle. It's my duty to inform you that if you were to accept the castle, you would also inherit two million Euros to help you take care of it."

Silence.

Say what???

Chapter 23

S ay what???" asked Kate on the phone.

"That's exactly what I said!" answered Amanda, "well, I thought I said it, but Mr. Perrier had to snap his fingers in front of my face to shake me out of it. Not sure I've really recovered yet though."

"Say what???" asked Kate again.

Apparently, Amanda wasn't the only one to be stunned by the incredible news. She lay on her bed while d'Artagnan was on the floor, eating a bone. Bronx was evaluating a potential jump from the top of the wardrobe, ideally placed above the dog's head.

"Damn! This story gets better each time I talk to you," said Kate.

"Kate, seriously, I don't know what to do."

"Oh, I do know!" said Kate. "You take the castle and the money, and you do whatever you want with it. Simple. Can you sell it?"

"Well, that's 'the thing.' I can't sell the castle for ten years from the moment I accept the inheritance. And apparently, there aren't so many people interested in living the luxury castle lifestyle anymore. Even people who had castles in their families for centuries want to get rid of them because they are way too expensive to maintain. They often sell them for one symbolic Euro. Can you believe this?"

"What? *David, do you want to go to France and buy a castle for one Euro and live there?*" Kate waited for her husband's answer for a few seconds. Instead, Amanda heard a little girl yelling *"Me, me, me! I want!"*

"Kate, come on, be serious. I have an important decision to make. It means a lot of changes in my life if I accept this inheritance. It's a big responsibility, and most of all, I know *nothing* about castles."

"OK. Let's keep it simple: do you like the village?" asked Kate.

"The village is really charming. It's just like I imagined old French villages from seeing pictures, reading novels and watching movies," answered Amanda.

"Good. Do you like this castle?" pursued Kate.

"The castle, hmm... after the first visit, I wasn't sure at all, but today I saw all its charm and beauty.

And the location by the sea is absolutely amazing. I believe d'Artagnan loved it too."

D'Artagnan stopped chewing his bone, rolled on his side and straightened his ears, staring at Amanda. *Are you talking about me? What are you saying about me?*

Bronx sent a nasty look to Amanda. *Yeah, and as usual, nobody wants my point of view! Just this dummy dog's opinion matters? Pff. I haven't even seen the place yet!*

"Alright. As you'd have millions of Euros—I can't even believe I'm saying this—you would invest them in the castle, right? So, what would you do with the castle exactly, besides renovations?"

"To be honest, I had started to think about it...

"Ah! You see."

"I'd turn it into a fancy Inn..."

"Great idea!"

"And why not, I could open my own restaurant too?"

"Oh my God! Oh my God! Oh my God! Yes!" Kate was probably jumping in her living-room.

"And maybe, one of the rooms downstairs could become a little antique shop?"

"Amanda, that's it. You have your answer. You already know what you want to do with this castle. Forget about these silly ghost stories, and start living your dream. Do you want to come back to Victoria and work at the Registrar's Office until you retire or do you prefer to live in a castle in France and make your dreams come true?"

"Well, when you put it that way..."

"Seriously, Amanda, why are you still hesitating?"

Amanda pondered this for a few seconds.

Oddly, both Bronx and d'Artagnan were staring at her, as if they were waiting for an answer too.

Amanda stood up and paced the room.

"All right. Today, I start living my dreams. Today, I dare to say 'yes.' Today, my life changes. Today, I become the owner of a castle in Normandy, France," said Amanda decisively.

"Hooray!" yelled Kate so loud that Amanda had to pull her phone away from her ear, *"David, we just won holidays in a castle in Normandy for life!"*

Amanda heard a thump coming from the room. D'Artagnan howled. She turned around. Bronx had succeeded in landing on his target: the dog's head.

Chapter 24

Amanda finally signed all the paperwork. Twelve pages at the bottom of which she lay down her first and last names below the date, Friday, April 13, 2018. Although she wasn't superstitious, she still hoped that it wasn't an ominous sign.

Mr. Perrier offered Amanda a broad smile and even a glass of champagne. They stood by a gueridon near the window in the notary's office. The room was brightened by the sun pouring in, something else to be grateful for. They raised and clinked their flutes, and drank with delight the bubbly nectar.

The notary had a good reason to rejoice too as he had gained a new client. Amanda had asked him to remain in charge of the d'Orvilly estate and he had gladly accepted. She didn't want to deal with the mountain of official paperwork and documents related to the property, nor fight with French administration that had such a bad reputation. If

Toinette d'Orvilly had kept him as his notary for so many years, the man must be good at his job.

It was done. Amanda was now the owner of the medieval castle. The d'Orvilly estate was hers, and she also had 2 million Euros in her bank account. Crazy. Realizing all this made her feel tipsy, and it wasn't because of the champagne. But she didn't want to lose one second of getting to the next stage: revamp her ancestors' castle. She was aware that a lot of work was needed to make her French dream come true the way she imagined it.

"Mr. Perrier, do you know of any construction company in the area that has a good reputation?" she asked, "I will need their services. I also would like to meet with an architect. The castle needs renovations, but as you know, I have this Inn business in mind so I need to meet with professionals to explain my project and see what's possible or not. Ah, and I should probably meet with a landscaper too. I'd really like to meet professionals as soon as possible."

"You know, as we're a village mostly surrounded by countryside, you'd have to travel three hours to the next big city if you want to meet with several companies and make your choice," answered the notary. "I'm afraid you have not much choice but to hire local people if you want to move fast. But I have three names for you: the only architect in the village is Delphine Montel, Auguste Barbon owns the construction company that has done all the major and minor work around here for decades, and I know of a young man who just started his landscaping business, Antoine Verroyer. I've hired him a few times to take care of my garden, and he did excellent work. I'd like to encourage him and send him new clients." The notary walked to his desk and opened a drawer to take three business cards that he handed to Amanda.

"Wonderful! Thank you so much, Mr. Perrier."

The notary took the bottle of champagne and refilled Amanda's glass. Although she held a hand in front of her to stop him, Mr. Perrier had already filled it. He raised his glass and tapped hers.

"Dear Amanda, I wish you all the best as the new owner of the castle. Here's to the success of your Inn project!"

Chapter 25

To be efficient, Amanda decided to meet all at once Delphine Montel, the architect, Auguste Barbon, the owner of the construction company, and Antoine Verroyer, the landscaper. They were all waiting for her at the arched gate of the estate, below the sign 'Domaine d'Orvilly.'

"Good afternoon, I'm Amanda McBride, the new owner of the castle."

They all shook hands, except for the tall, slim woman with a stern expression, who stepped forward from the group. She looked at Amanda coldly.

"Delphine Montel, architect. May I ask, Ms. McBride, did you buy the castle?"

"No, I didn't buy it. I inherited it."

There was an awkward silence, and a few sideways looks.

"Ah..." said Auguste Barbon, the owner of the construction company, a tall and robust man with a big mustache ending with pointy and curved tips, "are you related to the d'Orvilly's? Because, obviously, with your accent, you're not from here. I've been told you're from the United States?"

It appeared that news travelled fast in Orvilly-sur-Mer… but in the wrong way.

"I'm Mrs. D'Orvilly's heiress. I just arrived here a few days ago. But I'm from Canada, sir, not from the States."

"Ah," simply said the contractor who didn't seem to care a bit about this important detail.

"Anyway," continued Amanda, "I thought that it would be easier to meet with you all at once because I'd like to start some renovation work as soon as possible. I need to know what can be done or not with the property. Shall we start the tour?"

They all followed Amanda along the main path that lead to the castle.

"I plan to turn the castle into an Inn. I'd also like to open a restaurant and an antique shop."

Amanda noticed that the only one smiling and showing some enthusiasm to do the tour was Antoine Verroyer, the young landscaper.

"First, I'd like to have some landscaping done. Obviously, a lot of clearing is required because this estate hasn't been maintained for years. Some parts are even dangerous to walk on. I'd like to keep the trees, but would it be possible to arrange some nice flower beds to make this allee more welcoming?"

Antoine Verroyer scratched his head. "Sure, madam, I don't see why not. I could suggest a few possibilities. Do you have a preference regarding the flowers and the design you'd like to have on the front?"

"Not really... Could you do a few sketches for the design and give me a list of the flowers you'd suggest for the beddings, and then we'll see?"

"Sure, madam, I can do that."

"Now, as the castle will be turned into an Inn, I'll need parking for my visitors. Where would you suggest we build it, Mrs. Montel?"

The architect stopped and scanned the land from the gate to the castle. "The front gate being the only possible access to the property, I'd suggest setting a parking area close to the north side of the castle, on the far right. This way, your customers will be close to the edifice, but the parking lot won't look too obvious if you put it on the side. You can make this area look nice with some landscaping work, hiding it with shrubs maybe. Just a suggestion." She glanced at the landscaper.

"That sounds like a good idea," answered Amanda. "Now, let's go and have a look at the old garden in the back, and then we'll let Mr. Verroyer inspect the ground by himself for his landscaping work, while the four of us start our visit inside."

"Hmm, Ms. McBride," said Barbon, playing with his moustache, "just checking with you, but did you contact the mayor's office about the changes you're planning on making on this property? The municipal services office must approve any major changes you want to make. Or not."

Amanda blushed. "Oh, I have to say, no, I didn't... I feel stupid now. I hadn't thought of this at all, I'm sorry, I'm new here and—"

"Call the mayor," said the architect with a dry tone. Delphine Montel took a little notepad from her bag, wrote down something on the first page, tore it off and handed it to Amanda. "Here's his office phone number. There's no point in us wasting our time making this tour if the mayor isn't even aware of what you're planning on doing here. Call us when you get an approval. If you even get one."

The architect walked back to her car and left the property without even saying goodbye. Not saying a word either, Barbon waved a nonchalant hand and jumped into his truck, leaving Amanda and the young landscaper on their own in front of the main door.

Amanda was speechless. Were all Normans as rude as this when making business deals?

Embarrassed, Antoine Verroyer smiled shyly. "You shouldn't worry, Ms. McBride. These two have the reputation of being a bit... 'crusty.' But I'll gladly have a look at your property."

Chapter 26

Amanda was waiting in a chair, holding in her hands a file with important documents that Mr. Perrier had helped to put together within a few hours. She was nervous, tapping her feet on the floor. What if the mayor refused to give her a building permit?

She noticed the feet of the mayor's assistant, whose desk was a few steps away from her. The little light blue pompoms at the top of her flat shoes were bouncing as she was typing on her keyboard. A plaque with her name and her position, 'Joséphine Perrin, Assistant' was displayed on her desktop.

"The mayor will see you shortly," said the woman.

The door beside the assistant's desk opened.

"Ah! Ms. McBride. Come in."

The tall and hefty man with curly red hair gestured with his left arm to invite Amanda in his office. "Please, have a seat."

A crooked official portrait of the French President was hung behind the mayor's desk. The large desktop was covered with piles of files and papers, and the rest of the room looked like an attic. Everything seemed upside down. Amanda wondered how and why some of the items had landed in this office, like a bicycle wheel stuck between two piles of books. Apparently, the man had some issues getting organized... or he liked it better this way. Either way, it was far from the Canadian model of office management that Amanda knew.

"What can I do for you, Ms. McBride?" The mayor sat far back in his chair, making it swing back and forth, crossing his hands on his stomach, squinting and waiting for an answer.

"I'm Mrs. Toinette D'Orvilly's heiress. I just signed the paperwork to inherit the castle."

"Hmm, hmm," merely said the man.

"I want to start some work on the property as soon as possible. My plan is to transform the castle into an Inn, a restaurant, and an antique shop. But it needs considerable renovations before it can be turned into businesses and used as accommodations."

"Hmm, hmm."

"So I have prepared a file regarding the project so that you can have a look at it. I'm requesting a building permit."

The mayor took the file and opened it, had a quick glance on each page, closed it, and put it on his desk.

"The ghosts don't scare you?"

"Pardon me?" asked Amanda, a bit disturbed by the question.

"The ghosts."

"Huh... I've heard about these ghost stories, but frankly, Mr. Mayor—"

"Call me Charles. Everybody calls me by my first name here."

"All right, Charles. I've decided to ignore these ghost stories. I understand that they're part of the local folklore, but I can't base my decisions on ghost stories."

"Hmm, hmm..."

What kind of "hmm, hmm" was this? Good or bad? It was hard to read the man.

"Well, Ms. McBride, I don't see any reason why your request to start the renovations should be declined. Chances are good that they'll be approved by the offices concerned. You'll have to file more paperwork though. That's French administration. Always more paperwork and forms!" The man laughed loudly. His powerful laugh resonated in the office, and his joined hands on top of his belly moved as his body was shaking. "All right. I'll take care of this and will call you as soon as the papers are ready. You're staying at The Little Norman, right?"

Amanda looked surprised. Nothing could be hidden here. The village lifestyle, she guessed. "Yes, I am."

"Ah, good people, Régine and Paul. Good choice. I bet they're treating you well."

"Oh, yes, of course they are."

What other choice did she have, anyway? It was the only hotel in the village. The man stood up and accompanied Amanda to the door.

"No worries, I'll take care of this, little mademoiselle."

This 'little' again? Amanda was aware that she was only 5'3, but still, Orvilly-sur-Mer wasn't exactly a village of giants. Why did they all call her 'little?'

The Mayor closed the door behind her and Amanda felt relieved and surprised that all had gone so smoothly. So why did Delphine Montel, the architect, make it sound like it would be difficult to get the mayor's approval to start the renovation work?

Chapter 27

Two days later, Amanda received her building permit, and work on the property was scheduled to start in the last week of April.

On a chilly morning, humid but not rainy, two white trucks with the red inscription 'Barbon Brick and Mortar' were parked in front of the castle. Auguste Barbon barked orders to his twenty employees on site who had already begun to install high scaffolding along the castle's facade.

"I want everybody to wear their safety helmet and belt at all times," yelled Barbon, "no exceptions!" The man unrolled a large sheet of paper on top of a board on trestles beside the truck, and waved a hand at a worker. A short and chubby man with dark hair, probably in his early thirties, walked quickly toward Barbon. "Martin, take the new guys with you to clear the ground of this messy area over there. It will be the parking lot. I can't even walk there, I'm allergic to these damn weeds, so I'll let you deal with that. We need to clear enough for a surface of fifty feet by twenty minimum. Then install scaffolding on the side and on the back. And I'm not joking with the safety rules. Make sure you brief your young guys properly about this. You got me?"

Martin nodded and walked away, hands in his pocket. "Yeah, damn safety rules again..." mumbled the man. He joined a group of young men who were waiting for him, all in their early twenties. He told them to take some tools from the trucks and to follow him.

Meanwhile, Antoine Verroyer, the landscaper, was already working hard on the north side of the property, pulling up weeds energetically with a big rake, and accumulating them in a pile. The young man was panting. He paused for a few seconds to wipe his forehead with his forearm, avoiding carefully any contact with his gloved hands. Then he walked to his truck to grab a canister, and went back to his working area. He sprayed the weeds generously and put the canister back in his truck.

A black Mercedes entered the property, drove slowly along the main path, and stopped in front of the castle. Delphine Montel, the architect, stepped out of her car holding several rolled blueprints under her arm. She briefly shook hands with Barbon. Martin Plouque, who was just a few feet away from them, gave them a sideways look, and paid attention to their discussion.

"All is good here?" asked the architect.

"All is good," answered Barbon, "these are the new plans?"

"Yes." Delphine Montel gave the rolled papers to the man. "We should be fine. The changes shouldn't make a big difference. I suggest that you have a look at them right now and call me immediately if you have any questions."

The loud sound of an object falling on the ground interrupted their conversation. A panel of wood had fallen from the scaffolding, landing just beside the architect's car, missing it only by a few inches.

"Are you kidding me?" yelled Delphine Montel, running to her car and looking up at an employee who was standing on a scaffolding above the car. She checked her vehicle. It didn't have a scratch.

"Barbon! Brief your guys about safety *again*, dammit!"

"I did and always do!" barked Barbon.

The architect stepped into her car and left the property, driving fast on her way out, leaving clouds of gravel dust behind her.

Barbon grumbled and raised his head at the workers on the scaffolding, showing a threatening fist.

"I swear I'm going to kill you guys if you aren't more careful! How many times do I have to tell you about safety on site?"

The man kept mumbling while rubbing the tip of his mustache. "Stupid idiots..."

A taxi arrived and parked in the allee. D'Artagnan jumped out of the car, followed by Amanda holding a meowing pet carrier. The taxi driver went to the trunk and removed several grocery bags.

"Hello, Mr. Barbon!" yelled Amanda, smiling and waving a hand at the man.

"What the heck is she doing here, this one?" he muttered to himself. He walked toward Amanda. "I'm not sure it is a good idea to be here while we're working. It can be dangerous."

"You're working on the outdoors only for now, right?" asked Amanda.

"Yes, but—"

"Don't worry, I'll be inside for a short time, and I'll be very careful. I just need to do something that I haven't done for a while."

What the heck could that be that she has to do it here and now? thought Barbon, walking back to his table, mumbling and shaking his head.

The taxi driver followed Amanda to the kitchen, followed by d'Artagnan who couldn't help sniffing the grocery bags. The man put the plastic bags on the kitchen's counter.

"Here you go, miss."

"Thank you so much," said Amanda as she paid the man.

"Thanks. And good luck with the renovations!"

Bronx was protesting against his captivity with loud meows.

"I know, Bronx. Just a few seconds and you'll be free."

Amanda closed the kitchen door and put the pet carrier in a corner, and opened its door. D'Artagnan was watching Amanda, rolling his eyes.

No! Don't do that, please! Don't free this freak!

Bronx stepped out of the box and began to explore the room. The cat walked by d'Artagnan, touching him provocatively with the tip of his tail with a sadistic smile and a killer look. *One day, you will end in this little tiny box, and it will be the best day of my life.*

Amanda took her Ginette Mathiot cooking book out of her handbag and put in on the counter. She opened it and flipped the pages quickly. "Ah! Here it is... We're all going to stay in the kitchen for a couple of hours, and then we'll go outside to breathe some fresh air. All right?"

D'Artagnan looked disappointed. *Indoors, again? I hope that you have a good reason. Like preparing some food?*

Amanda emptied the plastic bags onto the counter: two dozen red apples, a box of eggs, a package of flour, a package of sugar, a little plastic bag with ground cinnamon, butter, sour cream, and a small bottle of Calvados. D'Artagnan sniffed each item carefully. *The meat? Where's the meat? Did you forget the meat?*

"I'm going to cook a traditional Norman apple pie, aren't you happy d'Art?"

No! I want meat!

"You're going to love this."

Bronx walked on the counter, looked with disdain at the items, then waved his tail in the air, in a very mischievous mood. *Why does nobody ever care about what I like?*

"I know what you're going to do Bronx. Don't do—"

Amanda hadn't finished her sentence before the cat gave a hard swipe to the apples with his paw, hitting them like golf balls with a club. The fruits rolled and fell on the floor.

"—it. Okay... I see that someone is still angry at me. That's fine. I get it. If I were kept in a box, I wouldn't be happy either."

The cat sat on the counter and watched Amanda pick up the red apples. *This is just the beginning.* Then he jumped from the table to investigate a wooden box left in a corner with empty wine bottles.

D'Artagnan frowned. *You, psycho cat!* The dog carefully stayed away from him, on the opposite side of the kitchen.

Amanda opened doors and drawers, searching for utensils, and found several pie plates in a cupboard.

"Bingo! Exactly what I need."

She started to peel the apples. D'Artagnan observed her carefully, hitting his tail on the floor impatiently, hoping for the pie to be ready within seconds.

"Good," said Amanda, "in about two hours, we'll have four delicious apple pies."

The Great Dane grumbled and lay on the floor. Bronx was licking greedily the neck of a red wine bottle.

Two hours later, just as she had planned, Amanda removed four apple pies from the oven. The apple slices arranged in a circle were perfectly golden, and the crusty pastry didn't break when she removed the pies from the dishes carefully. She cut them in equal parts, and displayed the pieces on a tray.

D'Artagnan stood by the platter with high interest, wagging his tail. *Gimme one! Gimme one! Gimme one!*

"I know what you want, d'Art," said Amanda, "but you have to wait a few minutes, it's too hot."

What do you mean, 'wait a few minutes?' I've been waiting for two hours already! Come on, this is torture! The Great Dane circled around the kitchen counter. He could very well stand up on his back legs and grab a piece of pie himself, but he knew Amanda wouldn't appreciate that.

Finally, ten horrible long minutes later, d'Artagnan got his piece of pie and swallowed it in one second. Then he sat like a good dog and looked at Amanda with sweet eyes. *More! Gimme more!*

"That's enough for now d'Art. These pieces are not for us."

The dog nearly had a heart attack. *What do you mean, 'not for us?!'*

Amanda took a small piece and looked for Bronx. She found him sleeping and snoring in the wooden box, holding onto a bottle of wine.

D'Artagnan frowned. *Don't you dare give it to him!*

"Well, I guess Bronx will have his piece later. Let's go outside, d'Art."

Amanda took the tray with the slices of pie and stepped outside, closely followed by d'Artagnan. She proudly offered slices to the workers during their lunch break while d'Artagnan watched in horror the pieces progressively disappearing from the platter. The men were delighted to see free desserts coming their way. Their eyes were wide open as the sweet bites of pie melted in their mouths.

"Yum... Thank you miss Amanda," said a worker, "it tastes wonderful!"

"Yeah," said another, "for someone who's not from here, you cooked it perfectly, like a real Norman. This apple pie is to die for, better than my mom's! Please, don't tell her that, she'd kill me!"

The men laughed, Amanda blushed.

"Well, I'm happy that you enjoy it. Here's more, I'll just leave it here for you."

Amanda put a large plate with pieces of apple pie on a trestle table.

"What's going on here?" Barbon approached with long strides, waving his arms. He looked at the platter. "The break is over. Back to work, guys."

"Would you like a piece of pie, Mr. Barbon?" asked Amanda.

"No, thanks. Maybe later." Hands on his hips, shaking his head, the man watched Amanda walk away with d'Artagnan towards the cliff behind the castle.

"What a grumpy man, this Barbon..." she muttered.

She sat down and looked at the ocean while the dog was running and smelling the ground. It was a gorgeous and sunny day. The air was a bit chilly, but the sun warmed her skin. She lay on the grass and closed her eyes, reflecting on her life, and how it had changed so quickly within a few weeks. She still couldn't believe it. Three squawking seagulls landed beside her, fighting over a piece of fish. They disrupted the peace on the cliff, but Amanda couldn't care less about the noisy birds. She was living her French dream.

Chapter 28

"**M**ademoiselle? Mademoiselle? Please, wake up."

Someone gently pushed Amanda's shoulder. She opened her eyes and put a hand in front of her face to block the sun. A man was talking to her.

"Oh, I'm sorry, I fell asleep. What time is it?"

"Apparently, you've been sleeping for three hours, miss."

"Three hours? Oh my God! Where's d'Artagnan?"

"Pardon me?" asked the man, intrigued. "D'Artagnan... The musketeer? As far as I know, he's still stuck in a book." The man laughed, content with his joke.

"No, I mean my dog."

"Ah. Just there."

Amanda turned her head. D'Artagnan was sitting by her side quietly, immobile as a sphynx. *I's about time! You're not going to like this.*

Amanda stood up.

"I need to ask you a few questions, mademoiselle," said the man. He was in his late sixties, of medium height with grey hair. He wasn't shaved and, oddly, was wearing a colorful Hawaiian shirt under his coat.

"Questions? About what?"

"Hmm... You're not going to like this..."

D'Artagnan squinted. *I already said it, man.*

Amanda was confused. "What? Who are you and what are you talking about?"

The man presented his hand to Amanda. "Oh, yes, my apologies, I forgot to introduce myself. My name is George Ferment, Judicial Police Officer."

"Judicial Police Officer?"

"Yes. I have a few questions about the deceased man on your property."

"A deceased... what?"

Amanda and the police officer sat in the lounge where Toinette d'Orvilly used to host her guests. They were surrounded by the golden leopards on the old tapestry. Amanda had the unpleasant feeling that they were staring at her.

"Mademoiselle, I'm sorry to inform you that a man was found dead on your property today, around 3 p.m."

Amanda was dumbfounded. "Sorry... Could you repeat that, please?"

"A-man-was-found-dead-on-your-prop—"

"No, I understood... What man?"

"A man named Martin Plouque. Do you know him?"

"No. I barely know any of the people here. Who is he?"

"He *was*, shall I say, one of Mr. Barbon's employees, working on the site. So, you're saying that you don't know this man at all? You've never met him?"

"No, I haven't."

"Hmm... It's odd. Maybe you don't know him, still, it appears that he ate *your food*."

Amanda's heart skipped a beat. "What?"

"We strongly suspect that this man has been poisoned. Not sure yet. Did you cook apple pies today?"

"Yes..." Amanda didn't like where this conversation was going.

"Well, apparently, this man has been poisoned, and it might have been by your apple pie."

Amanda's face turned white. "You must be kidding me!"

"No, I wouldn't, mademoiselle. This is a very serious matter."

A sudden worry darkened Amanda's face. "Oh my God! Are they all dead?!"

"Who?"

"The workers, out there, are they all dead? They all ate my apple pie. I think. Oh my God!"

"Hmm... it seems that no other worker is dead... not for now, at least." The man smiled slightly.

"Oh my God! I killed someone?"

"I didn't say *you* killed someone. I said that Martin Plouque died, possibly poisoned by something in *your* apple pie. There's an investigation going on now, and I'm waiting for lab results to confirm that."

"But what if it's confirmed?"

"One thing at a time, mademoiselle. You're staying at The Little Norman, right?"

"Yes."

"May I drive you back there? This property is now a crime scene and must be evacuated to let our experts do the investigation on the ground, and as you're one of the suspects, you'd better stay in the hotel for now."

Amanda was in shock. She followed the inspector without saying a word. Then she remembered about d'Artagnan and Bronx.

"Wait, I have to get my dog and my cat."

"Don't worry, we'll get them for you."

When they left the grounds, two police cars were parked at the front. Barbon and the workers were gathered and were being questioned by several officers. A policeman put handcuffs on Antoine Verroyer's wrists. The young landscaper looked at Amanda sadly when she walked by him.

Chapter 29

As if the forces of nature had decided to be in communion with the fatal event, a storm burst out on Orvilly-sur-Mer. Dark threatening clouds covered the sky and strong winds blew and whistled, provoking a symphony of banging shutters in the little village.

"I just became the owner of the castle, and someone got killed there. That's horrible." Amanda shook her head in disbelief, holding a little glass of Calvados that she had barely sipped, offered by Régine and Paul who sat in front of her in the hotel's dining room.

The couple was all ears, gulping their third glass of Calva. They had opened their best and oldest bottle of the famous local apple brandy that they kept preciously in the cabinet that dominated the dining room. The massive piece of furniture was a typical Norman buffet, an antique that had been in Régine's family for several generations. It smelled of wood and old cellar, and creaked loudly each time a door was opened. No burglar could escape with their cherished bottles of Calva. Régine and Paul had saved this one for a special occasion. They figured this was one.

"I'm not a killer! I don't know what happened. I just cooked the apple pies. I don't want to spend the rest of my life in a French jail, this wasn't the French dream I had in mind."

"Of course not, poor little thing," said Régine, holding Amanda's hand to comfort her. The woman refilled her glass. "Have a sip, it will help."

Amanda, who wasn't used to drinking strong alcohol, swallowed a generous gulp of Calvados and grimaced.

"You shouldn't worry, Amanda," said Paul. "George Ferment didn't say you were guilty, but that you're only a suspect while the investigation is going on. That's different."

"And this poor Antoine Verroyer who got arrested," pursued Amanda, "I don't believe for one second that he did this."

"Me neither," said Régine, "he's a good and respectable young man. I know his family. Very nice and polite people. Too bad for him, he had just started his landscaping business."

Flashes of lightening flickered. Titi got scared and rushed straight from his cushion under the Norman buffet to hide and shake. D'Artagnan sitting in the middle of the dining room wasn't impressed. *Yeah. That's what I thought...*

The bell at the front door signaled a customer stepping in. A tall man in a grey trench coat that dripped water on the floor generously, stopped in the entrance. He closed his black umbrella, put it in the umbrella holder, and removed his coat. The man's spotless white shirt, perfectly tailored black suit, and expensive leather shoes gave him a classic and elegant 'French Couture' look. He walked toward the reception desk with a very straight posture, carrying a little suitcase in his left hand.

Paul stood up and walked to the reception area to welcome him. "Good afternoon, sir, a room for one or for two?"

"Just for me."

"How many nights will you stay?"

"Three nights for now, but I might stay longer, I'm not sure yet... Can I confirm this later?"

"Of course, no problem, sir. Please fill in this form." Paul handed a pen to the man, but he took out a pen from an inside pocket of his suit instead.

"Can I pay with cash?"

"Sure, if you're willing to pay for the three nights upfront. Just as a guarantee, you know."

"I understand." The man slid his right hand under his vest to reach his wallet and gave five bills of one hundred Euros each to Paul, who couldn't help but notice that the wallet had a thick bundle of these.

Paul grabbed a key from the board behind him and gave it to the man. "Room 3, first floor, on your left, sir. Breakfast is served between 6 a.m. and 10 a.m. For lunch and dinner, please tell us ahead of time if you want to eat in the dining room. As this is the slow season, we only set the tables when requested. You can also order a tray and we'll bring it to you upstairs. If you prefer to eat out, there's a good bistro down the street, in front of City Hall, by the fountain, The Old Calvados. You can't miss it. Well, have a good stay, Mister..." Paul looked for the client's name on the form, "Mister Durant."

The man didn't say a thing and went up the narrow stairs, bending his head to avoid hitting the low ceiling.

Amanda's eyes followed the man as he was went up the stairs. Thunder rumbled, getting louder. A lightning bolt flashed hard and the walls trembled with the thunder that followed.

Chapter 30

I t was dark. Amanda could barely see around her. She was running in the castle from one room to another, following a woman who kept running away and hiding as if she were playing 'catch me if you can.' She could only see the bottom of her white dress. The rooms were rolling faster and faster, like an old carousel increasing its speed. Amanda's head was spinning.

"Stop!" yelled Amanda.

The carousel of rooms stopped. Amanda stood in the ballroom. It wasn't dark anymore; it was bright, very bright. The light dimmed slowly until Amanda clearly saw the whole room. It looked bigger than she remembered. Rays of sunshine passing through the four high windows gave the room the ambience of a summer afternoon. Surprisingly, the room was in excellent condition. The tapestry wasn't worn out and the deep brown of the fabric brought warmth to the room. The golden embroidery and the luster of the satin fabric added a majestic elegance to the space, and the magnificent chandeliers looked brand new. The reflection of the sun on their crystals produced magical sparks.

Then, an overwhelming yet wonderful scent spread throughout the room. It smelled delicious and sweet like cakes, pastries, cookies, chocolate, caramel, candies...

Amanda heard voices. The volume rose slowly. What sounded like one person at the beginning increased quickly as if people in an invisible crowd were talking. There was a funny thing about the way they spoke. It was French, but not exactly the French language that Amanda knew. People had an odd accent, pronounced words differently, and some words were unknown to her. They sounded like they were having a good time, with lively conversations and laughing.

And then, like a picture revealing itself, people appeared slowly. Fascinated, Amanda discovered a room full of men and women dressed in clothing from the mid-nineteenth century. Was this a costume party? It was definitely a party. The guests were eating delicacies and drinking champagne from flutes. In a corner of the room, three musicians were playing classical music. Strangely enough, nobody seemed to notice Amanda, as if she were invisible.

Two servants arrived on her right, pushing a cart gently with extreme care, on top of which sat a large, five-layer cake tower. The layers were round and white, decorated with tiny pink and red roses made of buttercream, placed on their circumference. Larger white roses decorated the base of the cake. The number 25, made of pink marzipan, sat on top of the cake.

Guests were in awe and stopped talking to admire the piece of culinary art. Positive exclamations rose in the room, then it went suddenly quiet. The crowd parted to let a young and elegant woman pass. She walked slowly toward the cake, dazzled by it. She wore a long and beautiful white dress. Amanda recognized the bottom of this dress. This woman was the one she had been running after. She was the woman whose portrait dominated the entrance of the castle. She was Mélie D'Orvilly.

Just before Mélie reached the cake, she stopped in front of Amanda and stared at her. She wasn't smiling anymore and had a tight expression on her face.

The young woman handed Amanda a teacup, exactly like the one that she had found in a bedroom of the castle. Now she could read the golden initials clearly: M.D.O. Amanda took the teacup. It was filled with tea, and little white flowers were floating on the top. It smelled odd.

"Amanda, if you don't wake up, you're going to lose us. Amanda, wake up now!" shouted Mélie d'Orvilly.

◈

Amanda woke up. "Lose who?" she shouted.

Surprised by this brutal awakening, Bronx fell from the windowsill. *What the heck, woman? You're the one yelling!*

Amanda put her thoughts together. She had had an odd dream, there was a woman in the castle, with a white dress, a murd— "Oh my God! Now I remember. I killed someone!"

D'Artagnan was posted by the bed, happy to see that his friend had finally woken up. *No, you haven't killed anybody, you silly. You are suspected of having killed someone. With an apple pie. Which was delicious, by the way. Please, make it again.*

Amanda stood up. The room heaved. Then, she remembered too that she had drunk a few glasses of Calvados with Régine and Paul the night before. "Oh, my... Why do people drink?"

As she walked slowly to the bathroom, leaning on the wall, the room phone on the nightstand rang. Amanda put her hands on her ears, moaning. She picked up the phone.

"Good morning Amanda," said Régine, "sorry to wake you up, I'm pretty sure you mustn't be feeling at your best right now, but Mr. Ferment, the police officer, just called. He said that he would like to see you as soon as possible at the police station."

Amanda moaned again. A hangover, a murder, and an interrogation at the police station. Could things get worse? Yes. Being sent to prison for murder.

"All right. I'll get ready and will go to the police station shortly. Thanks, Régine."

"Oh, Amanda?"

"Yes?"

"I have here waiting for you a big glass of water and a painkiller for your headache."

"Régine, could you please do me a favor?"

"Sure, what?"

"Please, avoid using the word 'killer.' Thank you."

"Oops. Sorry."

Chapter 31

Amanda waited in a little room, at a table, with an empty chair facing her on the other side. She could see her reflection in the two-way mirror in front of her, and was horrified to notice how awful she looked after her unfortunate 'alcoholic' evening. She couldn't figure out what she had tried to do with her hair, her skin looked dull—but the horrible neon lighting in the room could've been responsible for that—and she realized that she had put her shirt on inside out. She had the perfect look of a murderer sitting in an interrogation room. This didn't look good.

Mr. Ferment arrived in the room, slammed the door behind him, and dropped something on the table in a sealed plastic bag with a red label on it.

"Do you recognize this, Ms. McBride?"

"Oh, yes, this is my Ginette Mathiot, my cook book. I forgot it in the kitchen yesterday. Thank you."

Amanda was about to take her book back, but Mr. Ferment stopped her.

"Oh, no, no, no. Not so fast, mademoiselle. You can't have it back. This is a piece of evidence for the investigation."

Amanda froze, puzzled. The police officer frowned, staring at her with a stern look, holding the book on the table with one firm hand. Mr. Ferment looked much less pleasant than the day before.

"A piece of evidence?" said Amanda with a soft voice, "but, I don't understand, I—"

"Ms. McBride, you just recognized this book. Is *this* the one you used for your recipe?"

"Yes, but—"

"Oh. So, you admit it. Hmm... Show me the page of the recipe." Mr. Ferment removed the book from the sealed bag.

"Uh... If I well remember, it was on page 141," said Amanda while turning the pages nervously. "Yes, here it is."

"Perfect," said Ferment, "read it."

"What?"

"You heard me. Read it."

"I'm confused, Mr. Ferment, why should I read it? How will it help the—"

Mr. Ferment leaned on the table, adopting an odd and unsteady position, one hand on the table, and another on his hip. He was talking to Amanda, only two inches away from her face. "Please, don't make me repeat myself, Ms. McBride," whispered the police officer. "Just proceed."

Amanda was confused. It was quite a peculiar way to lead an interrogation. Were they all conducted this way in France? "All right," said Amanda, "'Norman Apple Pie for six servings. For the sugar crust pastry: one egg, two-hundred grams of white flour, one hundred grams of sugar, one hundred grams of butter, one pinch of salt. For the—"

"Stop there," said Ferment, "read the last part."

"Uh... Put in the oven and bake for 40 minutes?'" Amanda wasn't sure where all this was going. Mr. Ferment banged his fists on the table loudly. The table moved. Amanda startled.

"Exactly. For 40 minutes!"

She stayed silent for a few seconds, wondering if the officer had all his mental faculties. Or maybe she had lost hers? "Uh... Is there a problem with the 40 minutes?'" she asked tentatively.

Suddenly, Mr. Ferment straightened his back and gave her a broad smile. "How was it?" he asked proudly.

Amanda was bewildered. "How was... what?"

"This! Did I do good? Were you scared?" The police officer was waiting for Amanda's answer eagerly.

"Uh... Sure, you were quite... threatening..."

"Ah, great! I knew I could nail it."

"Mr. Ferment, I'm quite lost right now and I would appreciate if you could give me an explanation. What is going on exactly?"

"I wanted to impress you, like in these American detective movies, you know, when the suspect is in the interrogation room. I've always dreamed of doing this. I love these crime series we see on TV. So, I figured, as you're American, this was *my* moment, *my* opportunity to do it."

Amanda couldn't believe her ears. Was he kidding? "I'm not American, sir, I'm *Canadian*. So, I'm not suspected or accused of anything? All this was just... a game?"

"Yes! I'm in the drama club of the village. I just needed a bit of practice." The man put his hands on his hips, quite content. Then he frowned. "But if I were to accuse you of something, I would arrest you for your bad hairdo. Oh, by the way, your shirt is inside out."

It's not that Amanda didn't feel like jumping on the other side of the table to strangle the police officer to death, but as she was accused of nothing, she figured it was better not to commit any real crime in a police station.

Mr. Ferment offered her a cup of coffee and gave her back the Ginette Mathiot.

"I can have it back? It's not a *real* piece of evidence?"

"Of course not, it was just a prop. Fun, right?"

Fun? Damned French humor!

Amanda gave him a tight smile. "So, what happens now? What have you discovered about the murder?" she asked.

"Well, we know for sure that Martin Plouque was poisoned when he ate your apple pie. But it wasn't because of the pie. The other workers ate your pie, and they're all fine. We didn't find anything in the kitchen that would be grounds to incriminate you, and a lot of workers saw you sleeping on the cliff the whole afternoon. So, you're officially removed from the suspects list. The investigation must continue though, but I'm afraid that it will have to be without me."

Amanda felt relieved, that was probably good news... "Why? And who's taking on the investigation then?"

"I'm retiring and will leave with my wife in two days for Hawaii. We will stay there for a few months. You know, that is where they filmed Hawaii Five 0?

I'm a great fan of this series." The police officer started to sing the theme song of the old series. Very off-key. Amanda wondered if she was still dreaming or, rather, was having a nightmare.

"Anyway, the Judiciary Police Services in Paris have to name a new officer. I was the only one here, and as their services over there are already overwhelmed with many cases more important than this one, I'm afraid this file isn't their priority at the moment. The thing is, until the new officer is assigned, the investigation is suspended. Which means that the renovations at the castle must be interrupted."

Great. Some more good news. "And how long would that take before the new officer is assigned?"

"Hmm... About six months? At best."

"You must be kidding me!"

"Nope. You know, this is Fr—"

"French administration. Yes, I know! Is there anything I can do about it?"

"I'm sorry, I understand how upsetting it is, but I'm afraid there's really nothing you can do about it. The only thing you can do is wait."

If there was one thing that Amanda hated, it was exactly that, to stay still and do nothing. "Mr. Ferment, I travelled all the way from Victoria to Orvilly just for this castle. I need this work to be started now so that I can open my Inn in a few months. I can't wait that long!"

"An Inn? Oh, that's a great business idea... But no. Nothing you can do about it, little mademoiselle. Sorry."

Amanda paced in the interrogation room, mumbling, holding her cooking bible tight against her chest. The 'little' mademoiselle was *not* going to stay in a small hotel room for six months with her dog and her cat, she was *not* going to wait for the French administration to assign a new Judiciary Officer, and she was certainly *not* going to wait patiently to see what happens. Amanda wanted her French dream to come true, and for this to happen, she had no other choice but to find the killer *herself.* "Is Antoine Verroyer still accused of committing this murder?"

"Yes. He's the only solid suspect we have. And for him, it means staying in jail until this case is solved, unfortunately."

"This French administration is absolutely insane! I'm convinced that this young man is wrongly accused of this crime. Fine. I'll find the killer myself."

Mr. Ferment looked amused. "Ho, ho, ho! You can't play the private investigator like this, Ms. McBride. It's not as easy as you think."

After what she had seen? Amanda was willing to try. "Please, give me all the information you have about this case," said Amanda.

Mr. Ferment quickly grasped a file on his desktop. "I'm afraid I can't do that, Ms. McBride. This is confidential information."

"I won't give up, Mr. Ferment." Amanda got closer. "Was Martin Plouque in any sort of personal or professional trouble?"

The officer closed his eyes and crossed his hands over the file on his desk. "I can't tell you this either."

Amanda leaned over the desk. "What was in the piece of pie that killed Martin Plouque?"

The police officer remained silent as a stone.

"Come on! You must give me something," implored Amanda, "I'm not going to wait six months, doing nothing. Please, Mr. Ferment."

"All right, all right... Listen, if you help me practice my tough interviewer skills now, I'll give you a few clues that might be helpful."

"Mr. Ferment, you'll retire next week, why do you need to practice your 'tough interviewer skills?'"

"Oh, that's not for work. It's for the drama club. I'll be auditioning for a play this fall, just after my return from Hawaii. I have to pretend to be a tough American detective so I need to practice. And as you're American..."

Amanda closed her eyes and sighed. "*Canadian*, Mr. Ferment, I'm *Canadian*. Fine, I'll do it. But give me some information from your file, now."

"All right. I'll give you two clues, but you'll have to do the rest of the job yourself. I'll start with this one: Martin Plouque was poisoned with a deadly cocktail of pesticides that was spread on the slice of pie he ate. These pesticides all came from canisters we found in Antoine Verroyer's truck, which is why we arrested him. He's our only suspect so far."

"But there were more than twenty people on the property that day. Anyone could've taken these canisters and spread the pesticides on the slice of pie."

"I know. But we have no trace of handprints other than Verroyer's on these canisters."

"And what about Antoine Verroyer's motive to kill Martin Plouque? Did he have any reason to kill him?"

"That's another problem. Many people in the village had issues with Martin and hated the guy. So there's any number of people who wanted him dead. I know that Plouque had seriously bullied Verroyer when they were in the same secondary school. So far, that's our motive. Revenge because of past bullying."

"All right. So, what's the second clue?" asked Amanda.

"A name: Gisèle Poisson."

Gisèle Poisson? Who the hell was Gisèle Poisson? Amanda didn't know, but she knew someone who might.

Chapter 32

Liliane was stirring her spoon in a lovely pink teacup with a green handle. She had chosen 'Chat in The Morning,' a white tea with a mix of spices and fruits, while Amanda had ordered a large café latte, no sugar. The women had added a few chocolate cookies to their order. A visit to The Secrets, the tea and coffee shop on Brigadier Street, wouldn't be proper without little treats. Two ladies sitting at another table, a few feet away from them, were talking with the owner, placing their order.

"I'm surprised you're asking me who Gisèle Poisson is. You probably have met her already," said Liliane. "She's Mr. Perrier's assistant."

"Oh, yes, I've met her," answered Amanda, "but she never introduced herself. Why would she be of interest?"

"I'm not sure exactly why, but she's Martin Plouque's sister-in-law... Well, she was."

"Ah, interesting... What else can you tell me about her?"

"That she's the worst gossip in town. I don't understand why Mr. Perrier keeps her. With the important affairs he deals with in his business, she's probably the worst assistant a notary could have to keep his files confidential. I guess it must be hard to find someone with the proper training in a small village like ours. But her tongue has provoked many disasters in the past. Not only does she spread rumors she shouldn't, but she also adds lies to them. She likes to make things look bigger than they are, reveling in the dramas she creates."

"Hmm... I see. Did you know Martin Plouque?"

"Oh, yes! If you needed a guy to play bad tricks on people, you just had to go and find him. He's been involved in many scams and sordid stories, and unfortunately, he started them early in his life. I remember his poor mother always looking for him, scared each time her phone rang of learning about new offence he might have committed. When he was young, she had to pick him up regularly at the principal's office, and as he grew up, at the police station. Nothing could stop Martin from doing the wrong thing. There are people who are born like this, I guess... His mother was a sweet woman who never deserved an ungrateful son like him."

"What kind of bad things did he do?"

"Everything. Breaking into people's places, stealing, entering into bad deals, bullying and blackmailing people... Pretty much anything to cause trouble and make money fast. He also had a bad temper, so people were easily intimidated by him."

Amanda glanced at the other customers who were digging their spoons into two giant pieces of strawberry cake. She sighed. "I miss cooking... I can't possibly stay at the Little Norman for six months. Although I'm staying in the biggest room, it's still not big enough for me and my pets."

"Oh, how's Bronx, by the way?"

"He's... consistent. The other day, he escaped through the window. I ran outside in a panic to look for him, and found him in the arms of an old lady in the bakery, eating choux buns."

Liliane laughed. "Ah! That cat is quite something. And he seems to enjoy torturing you. Why is that?"

"He's never accepted d'Artagnan. He's jealous of him and makes me pay for it."

Liliane had a malicious smile. "So... You met the baker?"

"Yes." Amanda looked away.

"And?"

"And what?" Amanda blushed.

"Quite a handsome guy, right?"

"Yes... But I'm afraid I've made a bad impression on our first encounter."

"Why is that?"

"I was in my pajamas, slippers, and old sweater, hair undone, looking like a crazy woman who had just escaped from an asylum."

Liliane laughed out loud. "Oh! My dear... At least, there's one consolation: he *will* remember you."

Amanda smirked and sipped her coffee. "I wish it were not that way..."

"Don't worry, Amanda, you'll have another chance to give him a second impression, and a good one this time. Come to our monthly community dinner on Saturday evening. He's usually there and brings cakes and pastries for everybody. It will start at 7 p.m. at the Village Hall. Make sure you look nice. I'll pretend that I don't know you two have already met, and I'll make the introductions."

"So, I assume that he's single?"

"No, he has two wives and ten children... Of course, you little fool! Oh, by the way, if you can't bring a meal, you'll have to pay 5 Euros at the door."

"Me? Not bringing a meal? You must be kidding." Amanda looked at the clock hanging on the wall behind the counter. Ten minutes before noon. She munched her cookie and drank her coffee in one shot. "Ouch, my tongue!"

"Of course, it's hot," said Liliane, "what are you doing?

"I must catch this Poisson before noon."

"Very funny," said Liliane.

Chapter 33

"You just missed her," said Mr. Perrier, "Mrs. Poisson left for lunch. Is there anything I can help you with, Amanda? Is it related to the castle?"

"No, I just need to talk to Mrs. Poisson about something else."

Mr. Perrier frowned, wondering what Amanda would want to discuss with this wicked tongue of Gisèle Poisson. "You might find her at The Old Calvados. She sometimes has lunch there."

Amanda walked towards the door.

"Amanda!"

Amanda stopped and turned around, waiting for the notary to say something. Instead, he just bit his lips. "Hmm... nothing."

Gisèle Poisson was sitting at a table near the front window of The Old Calvados, dividing her attention between a gossip magazine and the action going on in the marketplace. All this while eating a traditional ham and butter baguette sandwich.

"May I?" asked Amanda.

Gisèle Poisson raised her eyes and looked at Amanda from head to toe as if she were a piece of dirt. "Ah. You're the little American."

"I'm Canadian. It's not the same. And I'm not so lit—"

"What do you want?"

Amanda pulled a chair and sat in front of Gisèle Poisson. The woman squinted.

"First, let me express my condolences for the loss of your brother-in-law, Martin Plouque."

"Hmm..."

"Would you mind if I asked you a few questions, Mrs. Poisson?"

"Questions? About what?"

"You see, I'm trying to figure out what happened the day your brother-in-law died."

The skinny woman pointed her long nose toward Amanda. "Why does it matter to you?"

"Well, it matters a lot to me because, as you know, I'm the new owner of the castle, but I can't have any renovations done there until the case is solved. And most important, an innocent young man is in jail, wrongly accused of this crime. I can't let Antoine Verroyer remain there."

"I'm afraid I can't help you with that." Gisèle Poisson went back to her reading.

"Maybe you can. As you might be aware, Mr. Ferment is retiring—"

"Yes, I know this, of course," said Poisson, keeping her eyes on her magazine, looking offended that Amanda felt the need to mention the obvious.

Amanda had to find something else to make her talk. She had to feed this Poisson with her preferred food: gossip or something that sounded like it. "Did you know that I want to turn the castle into a fancy Inn?"

"Of course, I know this."

Of course... there was nothing about this village that this woman didn't already know. Amanda tried something else. "I saw a ghost there."

Gisèle Poisson dropped her magazine. Her face lit up. "You did?"

It worked. "Yes. In the kitchen."

"In the kitchen? What was it doing? Cooking? Was it scary?"

"Mrs. Poisson, I'll tell you all about this, but first I need to know why Martin died, and who killed him."

"Fine. What do you want to know?"

"Was Martin in any kind of trouble?"

Gisèle Poisson chuckled. "Him? Always. That was the norm for him."

"All right, hmm... Maybe you know about something specific that would be helpful? Was he in trouble with anyone?"

Poisson hesitated a few seconds, but the pleasure to spread gossip was too strong for her. "What I'm going to tell you must stay between us. I'm not the kind to gossip, you know... And I don't want to be in any trouble with anybody. I could lose my job."

"Of course, I understand."

Gisèle Poisson leaned toward Amanda. "I know that Martin was up to something. But this time, it was something big. Bigger than the little petty thefts he was used to doing."

"Ah? What was it?"

"I've never seen him so invested into committing a crime. He kept saying that it was worth it, and that it was the big strike he had waited for all his life."

"Do you know what it was?"

"He told me that he knew something, crucial information, that made him realize that he could take advantage of some people."

"You mean that he blackmailed people?"

Gisèle Poisson looked sideways towards the window. "Yes. Something like that."

"Who did he blackmail, and why?"

Gisèle Poisson straightened her back. "I can't answer these questions, Ms. McBride."

"You can't or... you won't?"

Poisson sighed as if she were exhausted doing the job all by herself. She crossed her arms over her chest. "Just look into the casino, that's all I'm going to say."

The casino? There was no casino in Orvilly-Sur-Mer. What was she talking about?

Amanda stood up.

"Whoa, wait a minute," said Poisson, holding Amanda's wrist, "the ghost?"

"Ah, yes, the story about the ghost." Amanda sat back in her chair. Gisèle Poisson was all ears. Well, guessed Amanda, for a gossiper, gossip can't wait...

Chapter 34

D'Artagnan wondered why Amanda had spread all these paper notes on the floor. Was it a game?

"No d'Art, don't walk on them."

Why? wondered the dog, *it looks like fun to me.*

"So, what did you find out so far?" asked Kate on the phone.

"Well, I found out that our victim wasn't so much of a victim, but quite a bully and a criminal, and that he blackmailed some people in the community."

"Interesting. But who did he blackmail and why?"

"This is what I'm trying to figure out. His sister-in-law told me about a casino."

"Is there a casino in Orvilly?"

"No, so I did a little research online, and what I found out is quite interesting." Amanda read to Kate from her laptop. "This is an article from La Gazette d'Orvilly-sur-Mer, dated September 13, 2017:

Turbulent Meeting about The Casino Project in Orvilly-sur-Mer

Last Saturday, about three hundred residents attended a much-anticipated meeting at the Village Hall, all eager to hear about the Casino project submitted by the City to the French Lottery Organization.

Residents were divided in four groups: those opposed to the presence of any casino in the village; those not opposed to the opening of a casino, but disagreeing with the suggested location; those in favor of the opening of a casino at the suggested location; and a fourth group composed of seniors from the retirement home, Bellevue House, who mostly attended the meeting to enjoy the lively conversation, and eat the little canapés and mini-cakes that they declared to be 'much better than the disgusting food they serve at Bellevue House.'

After exposing the issue related to the Castle of Orvilly—whose heir or heiress hasn't been found to this day, six months after Mrs. Toinette d'Orvilly passed away—Mr. Perrier, the notary in charge of Mrs. D'Orvilly's estate, explained to the audience that the City and its residents had to debate upon the future of our local and historical heritage, in case no heir would be found in six months from now, deadline after which the estate would become public property.

The Mayor, Mr. Charles Desplanques, presented a project proposing to transform the old castle into a casino, about which he received both invective and applause from the audience. Explaining to our residents that an old edifice like the castle would be a costly venture that the City would not be able to cover, the Mayor and the City Council came up with the idea for this project. "A great opportunity to keep our local heritage while providing an efficient financial sustainability that would attract more tourists all year long, grow the popularity of Orvilly-sur-Mer, and change its image of a small village whose only notoriety rests on the vestiges of World War II.'

After these last words, the seniors in the crowd threw old carrots and tomatoes that they had kept from their lunch at Bellevue House at the Mayor and the Council members, booing at them.

After answering a series of questions, the Mayor and The Council invited the residents to leave specific comments in a box.

Coffee was served after the meeting, but the trays on the tables were already emptied of their delicacies. An attendee—who wishes to remain anonymous—declared 'the only good thing about this meeting was the canapés and the mini-cakes, and I'm leaving with some in my bag.'

Orvillians can visit the City Hall website to stay informed about the casino project. Another meeting might be held in a few months from now at the Village Hall, in case no heir will have claimed the inheritance of the d'Orvilly's by then.

"Well," said Kate, "at least we know one thing now: some people in town might not have been very happy when the notary found you."

"Yes, but I still don't understand why this Martin Plouque was killed. What did he have to do with all this? I have to find out who he blackmailed and why." Amanda took a closer look at her laptop screen. "Oh..."

"What?" asked Kate.

"There's a picture of the audience, just below the article, and I recognize someone there... This is odd. It's this strange customer who arrived in the hotel a few days ago... just after Martin Plouque was killed."

"This man is staying in the hotel *now?*"

"Yes. In the room just beside mine."

"That doesn't sound good, Amanda. Be careful."

Bronx walked on the papernotes on the floor and sat on them. D'Artagnan frowned, wondering why Amanda wasn't paying attention to him. *Why is this crazy cat allowed to sit on these papers while I can't even walk on them?*

Bronx smirked. *Mind your own business, silly dog.*

"It might be a good thing," continued Amanda. "Maybe this man knows something?"

"Yes... and maybe he knows too much," replied Kate, worried. "If he was in a dirty business with this Martin Plouque, that would explain why he's here."

"Hmm... One thing is sure: the village isn't that frequented at this time of year, so I'd bet that this guy isn't here by pure coincidence... I might be able to find out more about him. I'll call you back later." Amanda hung up and dialed another number.

"La Gazette d'Orvilly-sur-Mer, bonjour?" answered a woman on the phone.

Chapter 35

The rain rattling on the windows like a melancholic melody awoke Amanda who opened her eyes on a grey Saturday morning. It was raining ropes, as Normans say.

"Again?" said Amanda, "you know what, guys? I think Normandy beats British Columbia in matters of rainfall in a year, hands down."

D'Artagnan lay beside Amanda, hiding his nose under the blanket. *Agreed. Please, note that this weather makes me feel down. I'm not going out today.*

The bedroom felt cold and damp. Amanda jumped out of her bed, adjusted the thermostat, and ran to the shower.

After a few minutes, she was ready to leave, prepared to battle the rain with her red rubber boots on, a shirt and a sweater underneath her yellow raincoat, and a cloche hat too big for her head. She was standing by the door, playing with d'Artagnan's leash.

"Come on d'Art! It's just water."

The dog didn't move. *Uh, uh... As I said, not going out today. You go.*

"Fine," Amanda put back the leash on the dresser, "but the two of you stay quiet. Got it?"

Bronx answered with a 'meow' that sounded like a scary wry laugh. D'Artagnan gave him a worried sideways look. And for a good reason. Amanda had barely closed the door when the cat jumped on the dog.

Say your last prayer, 'd'Artie Honey!'

Amanda walked towards the pink reception desk of Bellevue House, the senior home in Orvilly-sur-Mer, and asked an employee wearing a pink blouse with the name tag 'Sofia,' to see Mr. Louis Lamour.

"Are you a relative or a friend of Mr. Lamour, madam?" asked Sofia.

"No. I don't know Mr. Lamour, but I'd like to talk with him about an article he wrote in the Gazette d'Orvilly a few months ago."

"One moment, please. Have a seat. I'll call his room and ask him if he's willing to see you."

Amanda sat in a large grey armchair facing the reception desk. The cushions were so soft that she sank low into them.

"What are you doing here?" asked someone with a dry tone.

Amanda raised her head. Mrs. Parmentier was standing in front of her, staring at her with a stern look. Amanda forced a smile. "Oh, Mrs. Parmentier, how are you doing?"

"As I said: what are *you* doing here?"

Was she the police of Bellevue House or what? Bad luck for Amanda.

"Uh... just visiting someone."

"Visiting someone, hmm? I bet you're lying. You know nobody here. Are you here to steal from us?"

"No! Of course not! Why would you think that?"

"Then what do you want?"

The woman was worse than a watchdog.

"Miss?" asked Sofia, "Mr. Lamour asks if you have food with you?"

"Uh, no... Am I supposed to?"

The receptionist spoke on the phone.

"How old are you?" asked the receptionist.

What? How was this question relevant?

"Thirty-nine," answered Amanda slowly, hoping this was the right answer.

"Fine. You can go up. Third floor, room 347, on your left once you exit the elevator."

Very happy to escape Mrs. Parmentier's tyranny, Amanda walked over to the elevator quickly, leaving little puddles of water behind her. Mrs. Parmentier didn't take her eyes off her.

"If you steal or do anything bad," yelled the woman, "I'll report you to management!"

Amanda felt relieved when the elevator arrived. She stepped into it with a short elderly lady who had been waiting beside her. The doors closed.

"Don't worry," said the lady, "she tries to boss everybody here. She's a former math teacher. Gosh, I've always hated math teachers..."

A bell rang and the little lady exited the elevator on the first floor, waving her hand and smiling at Amanda. "Have a good day, sweetheart!"

The elevator went two floors up. Amanda arrived on the third floor and walked down the long corridor. There were many doors on both sides, some of them open. A woman was watching television in suite 335, a man was singing in his wheelchair in suite 340, and a lady was standing by the door frame of suite 346, looking curiously at Amanda.

She knocked on door 347. Nothing. She knocked again. A caregiver pushing a woman in a wheelchair walked by.

"You have to knock harder. He's a bit deaf."

Amanda banged on the door with her fist.

"Yes, yes, yes! I'm not deaf! Come in!"

Amanda opened the door. A little man in his eighties, wearing grey pants, a flannel plaid shirt and suspenders was sitting in an armchair, a book on his lap. He removed his glasses, leaned forward and squinted.

"Who are you?"

Amanda presented her hand. "Good morning, Mr. Lamour. My name is Amanda McBride."

"Do I know you?"

"No, you don't, sir. I'm here to ask you a few questions about an article you wrote a few months ago for the Gazette d'Orvilly. If you don't mind answering them, of course."

"Do you have food with you?"

Decidedly, this was obsession.

"No sir, I'm afraid I don't."

"Ah. That's disappointing."

"But if you want, I can come back tomorrow and bring you some pastries?"

The man's face lit up. "It's a deal! What are your questions?"

Amanda pulled up a chair and sat in front of the old man. "Well, I want to talk about this meeting that was held at the Village Hall about the casino project. I assume that you were there that day, of course, as you wrote the article?"

"Of course, what a question! I'm a former journalist, I do my job professionally. If that's your question, I don't see the point of you coming here to ask me this."

"Oh, no sir, I have more questions."

"So, shoot because my bridge game is in thirty minutes." Amanda took from her bag the Gazette article she had printed. She showed the picture to Lamour, pointing her finger at the image of the customer who was staying at the hotel.

"Do you know this man?"

Louis Lamour took the paper and looked closer, squinting and making a face. "Nope. I don't," he looked at Amanda, "am I supposed to know him?"

"Not necessarily, sir. So, you really have no idea who this man is?"

"Miss, I might be old, but I still have all my mind. If I tell you that I don't know this man, I don't know this man."

"Of course, sir... So, besides the mayor and the council members, were there any other important people in the room that day?"

"Hmm... most of the people owning businesses in town were there."

"Would you say they were more in favor of the project or more opposed to it?"

"Like the rest of the villagers, they were divided."

"All right... so was there anything unusual that you might have noticed that day?"

"What do you mean? It was a big meeting, a lot was going on."

"Did you see anybody acting strange or people making odd comments. Anything that could be relevant. You're a journalist, I'm sure you notice these things very easily, better than most people, right?"

The man looked at the ceiling. "Hmm... Ah, maybe. The tall unpleasant woman, the architect, she was always with Barbon, the construction guy."

"You mean Mrs. Montel, the architect?"

"Yes, that one."

"And why would this be unusual?"

"Because these two like each other like cats and dogs. I'm not saying that they were smiling at each other, laughing together or something like that, but just the fact that they stayed together during the whole meeting, that was unusual."

"Interesting... And why do they hate each other?"

"Because two years ago a young guy died on one of Barbon's construction sites. Apparently, Barbon hadn't briefed his guys properly about safety. This is what Montel keeps saying, anyway. Unfortunately, the young guy who died was her son. He was only eighteen. Poor boy. Since then, she has hated Barbon. Very understandable."

"She didn't sue Barbon for negligence because of her son's death?"

"No. After an investigation, it seemed that the responsibility fell on the son himself because all the information and right equipment had been given to the employees working on the site. They never found out what had really happened to this poor boy that day, but for Montel, Barbon is and will always be guilty."

"I see..."

The man was getting impatient, tapping his fingers on his thighs. "Any other question? Because I have bridge to get to."

"No, sir, thank you very much for answering my questions." Amanda shook the man's hand and walked to the door.

"Hey!" said the man before Amanda opened the door. Amanda turned around.

"Yes?"

"I like the ones with apple sauce inside."

"Pardon me?"

"The pastries. You told me you would bring me pastries. I like the ones with apple sauce inside."

Chapter 36

Another storm swept over Orvilly-sur-Mer. Strong winds blew and whistled through the doors and windows. Amanda shivered, feeling a bit uneasy, standing alone in the damp kitchen in the castle. She wished d'Artagnan were here, but the dog had refused to accompany her. What if something 'odd' happened again? 'Ghosts don't exist, ghosts don't exist,' she kept repeating in her head.

She balled up several pages of old newspapers left in a corner and threw them into the fireplace, putting a few logs on the top. Then she took a box of matches from one of the grocery bags on the counter and lit up a big match, hoping that the wood would ignite.

Flames burned and grew slowly, giving a bit more brightness and warmth to the room. The outmoded light fixture on the ceiling was flickering. Hopefully, the power would keep working until she would be done with her cooking.

So she didn't waste a minute. She opened her cooking book and took out ten Camemberts and ten flaky pastry packs from the grocery bags on the floor, and put them on the large table, with the rest of the ingredients. She had to make a good impression on the Orvillians who would attend the community dinner that evening at the Village Hall. She hoped the Camembert puffs she would bring would do it. She noticed a paper left on the counter. She took it and read:

Dear Amanda,

We couldn't find the missing key to unlock the door in the kitchen, so we had to break the chain. You can now access the basement.

Mr. Perrier

Anxiously, Amanda turned around to look at the door. What if someone came out of that door? No. It was silly. 'Ghosts don't exist, ghosts don't exist... Right?' She decided to focus on the recipe instead. She opened the drawers and looked for a rolling pin. The door made a rattling noise. She stopped and looked at it. The door stopped moving. It was just the wind, probably.

Then she went back to inspecting the drawers and found a heavy wooden rolling pin that had obviously flattened a lot of dough in its time. As she unwrapped the flaky pastry, she heard a loud thud coming from behind the door. She was startled and stayed still for a few seconds. Her heart was beating fast. Why the hell had she decided to come here on her own? Maybe the heavy rolling pin would be helpful to use in case she were attacked, but as heavy as it was, would it still be useful to fight a ghost?

Silly thoughts. It was only silly thoughts. She needed these Camembert puffs. So she went back to the pastry and flattened it, working as fast as she could. "Just ten, ten Camembert puffs, quick, quick, quick, Amanda," she told herself as if she were singing a song, accompanied by the rustling of the trees in the wind.

The onions and the bacon were chopped with a big knife as fast as a chef would. She turned on the gas on the stove, grabbed a frying pan suspended from a hook, threw the pieces of bacon and onions in it, and poured a bit of olive oil all over them. All was going well. Then, a powerful blast pushed at the old window above the sink. It gave away and opened up, letting in the blowing wind and the heavy rain. The shutters swung, hitting the walls outside. Amanda rushed to close them and got soaked instantly. She battled against the blowing gale for a while, pushing hard on the shutters, managed to lock the window, and braced it with an old wooden box left on the floor. She sighed with relief and grabbed a cloth on the counter to dry herself off. She smelled something burning. "Dammit!"

She hurried to the stove to remove the frying pan from the burner. The onions and bacon that were supposed to be brown were a bit too dark and crusty, but not in a critical condition. She put them aside.

Then she removed baking trays from the oven and put them on the counter to place ten round flattened pastry pieces on them. She kept working at a fast pace, looking like a contestant on a show that could've been entitled 'How to cook in fifteen minutes what you're supposed to cook in sixty.'

She put the Camemberts halves, cut lengthwise, and all the ingredients on each round pastry, added some pepper, covered them with the other halves, and closed the puffs by crimping the edges with her fingers. Then she put the trays in the oven and lit a match to ignite the gas stove. "Done!"

Amanda set the alarm on her phone, and pulled a chair in front of the fireplace. She sat and reviewed the information she had gathered about the murder of Martin Plouque while the puffs were baking in the oven. A mouth-watering smell of cheese, onion and bacon spread in the kitchen.

Thirty minutes later, the timer went off. Amanda removed the Camembert puffs from the oven and displayed them carefully on the counter. Suddenly, the fire burning in the fireplace and the light fixture on the ceiling went off. Amanda stood in the kitchen in pitch darkness, petrified. She didn't move an inch. Then she felt a light wind brush against her cheek.

"Get *out* of my kitchen," whispered a woman to her ear.

Amanda yelled and the power came back. There was nobody in the room, but the door leading to the basement was wide open, revealing the steps going down to the dark cellar.

Amanda was trembling, holding onto the counter, too scared to move. 'Ghosts don't exist, ghosts don't exist…' Although she was losing faith in her mantra, she decided she wouldn't allow a ghost to rule her. It was her castle, after all, and she had the right to be here more than this ghost. So she took a deep breath, walked to the door and closed it, wishing Mr. Perrier had never unlocked it. Unfortunately, she couldn't find anything around to block the door.

The puffs with their golden domes were cooling on the counter. She hurried to put them in plastic boxes, gathered all her things and placed them in the plastic grocery bags.

Before she left the kitchen, Amanda turned around. "Make no mistake," she said out loud, "I'll be back."

Chapter 37

*W**Hat is that smell? I like it. What Did you cook?*

D'Artagnan followed Amanda who was pacing in her hotel room, speaking on the phone with Kate. The dog sniffed her hands and raised inquisitive eyes to her.

"I heard this voice, Kate. I swear, it was real!"

"Are you telling me that you believe in ghosts, now?"

"I don't know... maybe. I didn't make this up."

"I know, I believe you, but it's so creepy. Next time you go there, you'd better bring d'Artagnan with you, just in case. So, what did you learn about this weird customer staying in the hotel?"

"Unfortunately, nothing so far. I went to question the man who wrote the article in the Gazette, but he didn't know him. He gave me some relevant information about Montel and Barbon though, and I believe that I should dig into this a bit more. In fact, this is exactly what I'm planning on doing tonight."

"Ah, you're talking about this event at the Village Hall, right?" Kate switched to dulcet tones, "what will you wear to please Mister Sexy Baker?"

"Very funny, Kate... I didn't come here to go ballroom dancing, so I don't have fancy clothes with me. I just have a few jeans, some shirts, and a couple of sweaters, mostly."

"Gosh! How many times have I told you that you seriously need to revamp your wardrobe? Don't you even have a nice blouse?"

Amanda opened her closet to have a glance at the five simple pieces of clothing that were sadly hanging there among thirty unused hangers.

"Hmm... Ah, maybe. I have a white blouse. Simple, but nice."

"Jeans and white shirt, not bad. Wear them and make an effort with the makeup and your hair, and it should do it. You're pretty enough to make it work. Are you going to do it?"

"Yeah, yeah... " Amanda sighed.

"With more enthusiasm, please, it'll work better. All right, have fun tonight introducing people to your Camembert puffs. I have to go. There are three ogres here who are waiting for their breakfast."

Kate hung up. Amanda looked at d'Artagnan, sitting on the floor. Bronx was hiding maliciously behind a sheer curtain, observing them, persuaded that they couldn't see him.

"OK, guys, you'll be my fashion judges."

The pets didn't react.

"I see. Thanks for the help."

Amanda went to the bathroom and closed the door.

Chapter 38

Trotting along the dark streets of Orvilly and facing the strong winds that thrust her backward, Amanda was holding tight to the hood of her raincoat with one hand, pressing a large plastic box containing the Camembert puffs against her body with the other. She stopped at an intersection. Should she turn right or left? Damn. What did Paul tell her?

French villages were built like labyrinths. The irregular and narrow streets went in all directions, and took unexpected turns; very much unlike the square and simple North-American system that Amanda was used to. She stood at the corner, trying to read the blue street signs. One of them was so old that she could barely read the letters that time had blurred. The sound of steps slapping the rainy sidewalk distracted her attention. A few feet away behind her, a tall and slender man with a black coat and a hat was approaching at a fast pace. Amanda recognized the mysterious customer from the hotel. He was getting closer, staring at her. She felt the urge to make a decision. Right. Now she remembered.

Amanda turned to her right and increased her speed, checking over her shoulder to see if the man was still following her. He was. She walked as fast as she could, wondering if she should run instead. Would it look suspicious? Who knows, maybe the man would run after her and try to catch her?

As she was going up the hill, Amanda saw a building that looked like an old farmhouse. Two lit up lanterns hung on both sides of the main door were dancing and swirling in the wind. Several cars were parked around the building and people were walking hastily to the porch, some of them carrying things in their hands. She had found the right place.

Amanda felt relieved and safe when she finally stepped into the Village Hall. She was soaked from head to toe, but her Camembert puffs were safe. The place was crowded, and a lot of people were in line, waiting to buy their admission ticket.

"What does she have here, our little Canadian?" asked Régine sat behind a table, collecting money and giving away the tickets.

"Ten Camembert puffs," answered Amanda proudly.

Amanda put the plastic box on the table and removed her raincoat to hang it on a rack behind her. Régine opened the box.

"Hmm... They smell delicious, my dear. OK, no need to pay. Here's your ticket."

Régine leaned toward Amanda "keep it preciously because there will be a draw at the end of the evening. You could win a nice bottle of Calva." The woman winked.

Amanda shoved the ticket in her jeans pocket, took her plastic box and turned around to walk into the main room, banging the arm of a woman who was holding a glass of red wine. The wine flew out and ended its course on Amanda's white blouse. The only piece of nice clothing that she owned, which looked somewhat elegant, had turned into a bloody red disaster.

"Be careful!" protested the woman.

"Sorry," answered Amanda.

She apologized a dozen times, having to push people here and there to make her way through the busy Hall to reach the bathroom. She was stopped by a familiar voice, in the middle of the crowd.

"I told you to dress nice!"

Liliane was standing in front of Amanda with a dismayed look.

"It looked nice a few seconds ago, I swear," said Amanda with a sorry face.

"What happened to your blouse? Why are your hair so flat and your makeup running all over your face?"

"What? My makeup is running all over my face?"

Amanda brushed the black smudges of mascara underneath her eyes. She sighed. Crazy and messy wasn't the look she had aimed for.

"It's pouring and windy outside, didn't you notice? And, obviously, I had a wine accident."

Liliane took the plastic box from Amanda's hands.

"Go to the bathroom and clean this up, quickly. I told Pierre that I'd introduce you as soon as you arrive."

"Who's Pierre?" asked Amanda.

"Pierre Sablon, the baker, you silly! Go, go!"

"Oh my God!" Amanda ran to the bathroom, knowing very well that there was only so much she could do to fix this issue. Wine on clothes is a killer. She pumped the yellow soap from a dispenser that was nearly empty and rubbed it on her blouse energetically. What was red turned pink, and the stain spread all over her chest. She had to stop this.

She leaned toward the little sink and bent her body in an awkward and uncomfortable position to reach the tap. She spread water on her blouse, drizzling some on the floor. Two women arrived in the bathroom and gave her sidelong glances. Amanda smiled in return, feeling embarrassed and ridiculous to offer the view of her buttocks to the visitors. The women pretended to ignore her, did their business and left, whispering to each other.

The only thing that Amanda could see in the mirror was this giant pinky-soapy stain that covered the front of her blouse. It was definitely ruined, and so was the hope of looking glamorous in front of Pierre, the sexy baker. She gave up. It was time to dry this up.

She rushed to the hair dryer, bent backward under it and switched it on. As she was contorting her body to adjust her position to make sure that the air was directed toward her chest, a little girl entered the bathroom, stopped to look at her, and ran away. Great. Now she scared children and this damn thing would take hours to dry. The situation was ridiculous. So she gave up on the drying too and checked herself in the mirror again. She tied back her hair and wet a paper tissue to remove the black traces of mascara running down her cheeks. The little girl came back with a woman holding her hand.

"It's her," whispered the little girl to the woman, pointing at Amanda.

Amanda forced a smile.

"Go, quick," said the woman to the child.

The little girl ran in a toilet compartment. Her mother was staring at Amanda.

"Bad weather outside, hey?" said Amanda.

"Uh-huh," answered the woman, who didn't seem to be in the mood for a conversation with a crazy stranger.

The mother and her daughter left while Amanda was still standing in front of the mirror, feeling desperate about the situation. What other solution did she have? She could spend the evening in the bathroom... No. Liliane would come and get her at some point, or she would be kicked out of the Village Hall, known forever as the 'creepy little Canadian who hides in the bathroom.' She came to the conclusion that she had to assume that she'd probably be the worst dressed woman ever for an introduction to a potential date.

She walked toward the door and was about to leave the bathroom when she heard a man talking in the corridor.

"He knew too much so it was time to get rid of him..."

Amanda hid behind the door and gave ear to the conversation.

"... The deals don't change and the police investigation being suspended is a good thing... There are still a few things I need to do so I'll stay here a few more days... I'll call you if we need to change our plan. If so, I'll take things in hand myself."

Amanda tilted her head to better see the corridor. The man from the hotel was standing there, talking on his cell phone. Was he following her again? He ended his conversation and turned around as if he had felt a presence behind him. He saw Amanda's head and squinted. She quickly moved back her head behind the door. Had he seen her? She remained still for a few seconds, hoping that he'd leave. Then she heard him step away. She checked the corridor. It was clear. She scurried back to the Hall.

"What took you so long?" asked Liliane. "Oh my God! This doesn't look any better. Take this."

Liliane wrapped a long red scarf around Amanda's neck, letting it fall on her chest to hide the stain. Amanda grimaced. It smelled like old pungent perfume, maybe rose or patchouli.

"Lose this face," said Liliane, "smile!"

"Good evening, ladies."

The sexy baker was smiling, showing his perfect white teeth. Hot and irresistible in his blue shirt and jeans, he looked like a fashion model.

Are all French bakers that handsome? Wondered Amanda. If yes, she could become addicted to baguettes.

"Ah, Pierre," said Liliane, "let me introduce you to Amanda McBride. Amanda, this is Pierre Sablon, our wonderful baker."

They shook hands. Amanda blushed and smiled, thinking that she must look ridiculous with this big scarf around her neck while it was hot in the room. Liliane disappeared in the crowd, pretending that she had to go and speak to someone.

"So, we meet again. Do you have a cold?" asked Pierre, pointing at her scarf.

"No, I... I just twisted my neck last night."

"I hope it doesn't hurt too much. How's Bronx? Has he attempted any escapes again? He's quite a funny cat."

Amanda chuckled. "I wouldn't describe him as 'funny,' but he can certainly be entertaining at times."

"Liliane told me that you also have a dog?"

"Yes, a Great Dane, d'Artagnan. Although he's a lovely and funny dog, he and Bronx often fight. I'm never sure who started the war first or why, but I'm afraid their feud will never end."

"Maybe they secretly love it. You named your dog d'Artagnan, so I guess that you like Alexandre Dumas' book?"

"I do, but I have to say that I prefer to watch the movies based on The Three Musketeers."

"Do you have a preferred version?"

"Yes, the French one from the early fifties."

"Good choice. I believe this one is a cult movie. As news spread fast here, I won't conceal that I already know that you inherited the old castle. I also heard about the murder. I'm sorry about this, it's horrible."

Their conversation was interrupted by the voice of a man yelling and tapping a microphone. The sound was very loud and there was a high-pitched feedback. People in the Hall complained, and some of them put their hands on their ears. A man was standing on a little stage at the other end of the hall, holding the microphone. Amanda recognized Gérald, the man from the bar who had mentioned the ghosts in the castle.

"One, two, one, two... It works," said Gérald.

"Yes, we know!" yelled a man in the crowd. The assembly laughed.

The mayor stepped onto the stage and Gérald gave him the microphone. "Good evening, my dear fellow Orvillians!"

The citizens gathered in the hall shouted and whistled.

"I'm glad to see you here in such a large number tonight. There are a few faces here that I haven't seen for a while. Where have you been hiding?"

The audience laughed.

"We're going to share another great evening together, with good food, good drinks, and good music. But before we do so, I would like to ask you to observe one minute of silence in the memory of Martin Plouque who tragically lost his life this week."

The mayor and the room went silent. Amanda heard someone behind her whispering "a minute of silence? What a joke! This man was a real pest." Another person chuckled. Some people shushed them.

"Have respect for the dead!" said an elderly lady.

Amanda noticed Auguste Barbon and Delphine Montel, a few feet away from the stage, whispering to each other. The man kept scratching one of his forearms.

"All right!" said the mayor when the minute of silence ended. "Now let the fun begin. Please welcome on the stage the amazing band The Accordion Killers!"

People applauded and whistled to welcome the three accordionists who appeared from behind the black curtain of the small stage. The musician in the middle walked toward a microphone stand placed at the front of the stage, and began playing the introduction of a famous Valse Musette. Simultaneous exclamations of joy sounded in the room. The other musicians joined him after a few seconds. Couples started to gather on the dance floor.

"Do you know how to dance a Valse Musette?'" asked Pierre to Amanda.

Dancing? If there was something Amanda did *not* master at all, it was definitely dancing. "Uh... I'm afraid not."

"No problem," answered Pierre, "me neither. But we could try? It's like a waltz, but faster. We just have to follow people around us. And it's not a contest, so nobody will notice how bad we are."

Amanda laughed and offered her hand to Pierre. Getting closer to him, she noticed that the baker smelled like warm bread.

They joined the group of dancers, turning in circles in the center of the room. The pace was too fast for Amanda who had trouble figuring out where and when to place her feet appropriately.

"Wow," said Pierre, "I think you're a worse dancer than me!"

"Thank you so much for the compliment," answered Amanda, "I feel so confident right now."

Pierre laughed and lifted Amanda's arm to make her spin like a ballet dancer.

"Not sure that's a Valse Musette move, Pierre. I don't see anybody else doing this."

"I don't care," answered Pierre, "I just do what inspires me."

They bumped into a few couples of dancers who gave them nasty looks.

"Take lessons!" hissed a guy, who disappeared with his partner in the dancing crowd.

"Pierre, are you from Orvilly?"

"No. I moved here two years ago. I'm a Parisian. I had had enough of the speed and stress of the Capital. I happened to visit Orvilly a few weeks after the long-time baker had died. I was just taking a few days off to relax, but the villagers were looking for another baker. So, I jumped at the chance—if I can say so—and bought the bakery from his wife."

"Funny," said Amanda, "in a way, we have something in common. It looks like dead people lead us both to Orvilly. So, there's not one fiber of Norman in you?"

"Not a bit, as far as I know. What about you?"

Amanda was boiling. The dance floor was so packed that she could feel the heat and sweat of the dancers around her. She and Pierre were moving fast, trying to follow the music. The large scarf around her neck wasn't helping. "I was born and raised in Victoria, in British Columbia, a province in Canada. Have you ever been there?"

"No. Never been to Canada. But I've heard only good things about it. So how are you related to the d'Orvilly's then?"

Amanda did a fun move, twisting her back and bending her knees. It looked like a curtsy. "Toinette d'Orvilly was a great-great-cousin on my mother's side. It was a real surprise, not to say a shock, when I learned about this inheritance. I didn't know anything about my French origins. The funny thing is that I've always being passionate about French cuisine and French culture. And two weeks ago, I learned that I had inherited this castle in Normandy! And here I am. It's crazy."

Pierre did a little pirouette. Amanda was unsure what Pierre was trying to accomplish with this, and neither did the people around them who looked at him, amused. "Totally crazy, I agree. It must cost a fortune to maintain an old castle like this one though."

"Yes, it does... Did you know Toinette d'Orvilly?"

"In the last month before she died, I barely saw her. But in the months before that, she sometimes came to the bakery to buy bread and pastries. She particularly liked chouquettes."

"'Chouquettes?' What are 'chouquettes?'"

Pierre laughed. "The little buns covered with sugar that Bronx devoured the other day."

"Ah! I see. Well, he and my great-great-cousin seem to have something in common then. Was she a nice person?" Amanda stepped heavily on Pierre's right foot. He refrained from moaning and grimaced instead.

"Hmmpff... I remember her as being very discreet and polite, but reserved. Probably because of her education, you know, she was French nobility. At least, she didn't take part to all the drama and gossip going on in the village, like the seniors from Bellevue House love to do. They are so bored that it's literally their hobby."

"So, did you hear any gossip about the casino?"

"The casino?"

"I read an article in the Gazette about the project of building a casino in Orvilly. The castle was a potential location for it. Do you know anything about that?"

"Ah... yes. I remember now. It made a big splash. The kind that delights the villagers. It added fuel to the fire that was already burning."

"Which fire?" Talking about fire, Amanda had the feeling that one was burning inside of her. She had to remove this damn scarf as soon as possible.

"Mostly between the mayor and the architect, Delphine Montel. Do you know her?

"Yes, I've met her. I thought she got on well with the mayor?"

"It's not what I've heard."

"What did you hear?"

"Something about new contracts and money, I think. I don't know much more about it," Pierre did a rock'n roll flip, "am I wrong or are we gossiping too?"

"We might be gossiping, but I'd rather call it investigating."

"Investigating what?"

"I need to find out who murdered Martin Plouque. If not, I won't be able to start the renovation work in the castle for months, maybe not even till next year. I want to turn the castle into an Inn. That's my plan."

"Cool plan! If you need pastries and bread for your future guests, I'd be happy to provide them."

The music stopped for a few seconds, then the band carried on with another Valse Musette with a higher tempo. More people joined the dance floor.

"I don't know about you, Pierre, but I need to make a pause and eat."

"Good idea." He gave Amanda a radiant smile. "We'll go back ridiculing ourselves later."

"We looked ridicule?"

"Absolutely."

"So, how is it going?" whispered a voice in Amanda's ear.

Liliane was standing behind Amanda, all smiles, waiting for some exciting updates.

"Were you spying on us, Liliane?" asked Amanda.

"Of course, I was."

"Liliane, I can't keep this scarf around my neck. It's way too hot here. It's insane."

"What are you doing with my scarf, you little thief?"

Germaine Parmentier was standing in front of Amanda. The woman had a plate full of food in one hand, and a threatening fork in the other.

"Is it your scarf?" asked Amanda.

"Yes, it is," answered the woman. "Where did you get it?"

"Germaine, I'm so sorry," said Liliane, " I thought you wouldn't mind if I borrowed your scarf. I apologize."

"You didn't borrow it, Liliane. *She* stole it." The old lady was pointing her fork toward Amanda's face.

"This is a misunderstanding, Mrs. Parmentier," said Amanda. "I can assure you that I had no intention of stealing your scarf. I didn't even know it was yours." Amanda removed the scarf from her neck and handed it to the woman. "Here it is. I'm so sorry about this."

"My hands are full, you idiot. What do you want me to do with my scarf now? Put it back where it was, with my coat on the rack over there. You didn't empty the pockets of my coat, did you?"

"Of course not!"

"No worries, Germaine," said Liliane, "I will put back your scarf on the hanger with your coat. It's my mistake, not Amanda's. I thought you wouldn't mind."

"Well, I mind. I mind a lot! You, horrid little Canadian." The old woman returned to the crowd, managing to eat from her plate while complaining.

"Great!" said Amanda, "she hated me already, so now I guess that she wants to kill me."

"Don't worry about her. She's like this with everybody."

"Then why did you pick her scarf?"

"I didn't know it was hers. I just picked the first one I saw on the coat rack. It was just bad luck." Liliane walked into the crowd with the scarf in the direction of the coat racks.

"Ah! So that's what it was about!"

Pierre had finally discovered the hidden disaster, and the reason for the scarf cover-up.

"Red wine?" he asked.

"Yep," answered Amanda, "now that I'm officially and publicly ridiculed, please, pour me a glass of wine. I'd like to drink one, this time."

Pierre complied, smiling.

"You know, red-pinkish is a color that suits you well though. But I wouldn't recommend patchouli as a fragrance. Too old fashion for you."

Amanda smiled, happy that Pierre didn't seem to care about the mess.

Liliane took a big bite of the Camembert puff that she was holding in her hands. The cheese, the bacon and the onion flavors melted in her mouth, bringing a blissful smile to her face.

"Hmm, Amanda, this is delicious. You cook like a real Norman!"

"Thank you, Liliane," answered Amanda, proudly.

The two friends were eating and drinking, sitting on two chairs placed along a wall, facing the dance floor that had not emptied since the beginning of the evening. Some dancers who had obviously been drinking too much were making a comical spectacle, forgetting about their Valse Musette moves.

Pierre was dancing with a little girl whose feet were on top of his. She was laughing and her pigtails jumped to the rhythm of the music each time he moved his legs.

"Liliane, I need to ask you something," said Amanda.

"What?"

"About the mayor, Barbon and Montel. It seems that these three don't like each other, right?"

"Hmm... Not exactly," Liliane took a sip from her glass of apple cider. "Barbon and Montel hate each other, the mayor and Montel hate each other, but the mayor and Barbon have been close friends since childhood. These two always support each other, to the point that I can tell you that it's not only Desplanques who rules this village. Barbon has a huge influence on him. Therefore, he also has a big influence on all the important businesses going on here. It's thanks to him that Desplanques has been the mayor of Orvilly for over twenty years. More than half of the residents here listen to Barbon religiously, and he keeps them voting for Charles Desplanques as their mayor."

"So, he could've had an influence on this casino project?"

"Yes, I suppose so. Like he does for any major construction work in Orvilly. And the casino would've been a big one. Barbon was building up the excitement around it among the villagers because they were really divided. But when the notary, Mr.

Perrier, found you, then there was nothing to be excited about anymore."

"So, Barbon could see me as a 'problem?'"

Liliane's attention was focused on a quiche placed on a table nearby, wondering if she had enough room in her stomach to take a piece of it. "He could. But you don't just decide to build a casino like this. The French National Lottery would've had to approve it. Convincing the villagers was just the first stage. No one knows if the project would've been approved."

"But it could've been approved? Liliane, I believe that Martin Plouque might've been involved in this casino project, one way or another. Do you see that man over there?"

Amanda pointed to the mysterious man from the hotel who was standing in a corner on the other side of the room, observing the crowd.

"Yes... Why?"

"Do you know him?"

"No. I've never seen him here."

"Well, in fact, he has been here before. He was in a picture taken for the article about the casino in the Gazette d'Orvilly. He was here, in this hall, with the residents and the mayor when the project was discussed. Don't you find it odd?"

"Hmm... I don't know what to think of it. Maybe it's just a coincidence?"

"Maybe not. When I was in the bathroom, I heard him having a conversation with someone on the phone. He was in the corridor. He said that someone 'knew too much about something, so they had to get rid of him.' He must've been talking about Martin Plouque. He also mentioned some 'deals,' and finding it helpful that the police investigation was suspended. That can't be good."

"No, you're right," said Liliane, looking at the man, "but just a phone conversation doesn't make him a killer."

"I need to find out about these 'deals.' Martin Plouque knew something about these deals for sure, and maybe this is what got him killed. He was blackmailing someone. I need to find out who and why."

"Good luck with that," said Liliane, "most people standing in this hall have been blackmailed by him and hated him. It could've been any of them."

"Yes, but this time, Martin Plouque went too far. Liliane, I'm pretty sure that someone in this hall *is* the killer."

The quiche in Liliane's mouth tasted bitter. The woman looked at the crowd of happy villagers celebrating. She knew all of them. A chill ran down her spine.

"Number 2-1-2-5."

The villagers were silent, holding their tickets and reading them carefully, all wishing that this number was theirs. Most of them expressed bitter disappointment, except for one person who yelled for joy and ran to the stage.

"It's me! It's me!" yelled Régine.

She grabbed the gift basket and showed it triumphantly to the audience.

"And we can applaud our winner," yelled Gérald into the microphone, "Régine Beaudoin, who'll go home tonight with this amazing gift basket filled with foie-gras, ham, chocolate truffles and a good old bottle of our famous Calvados!"

"That's suspicious, she always wins," protested a guy behind Amanda, "the games are rigged!"

"And now, the last dance of the evening," continued Gérald, "a little Slow number before we all go to bed."

Only three couples were left standing on the dance floor, looking tired, hugging each other, and barely moving. One man stood still in the middle, holding an empty bottle of cider in his hand, eyes closed. His body was swinging forward and backward. He might've been already asleep.

The villagers slowly emptied the hall, waiting in the queue at the coat racks. It was still raining outside, and people had to fight with the main door when they opened it, battling against the wind.

Liliane and Amanda walked together along the streets of Orvilly, accompanied by Pierre who was the first to part ways.

"Have a good night, ladies. It was a pleasure to see you again, Amanda." Pierre offered another of his wonderful smiles and opened the door beside the bakery that led to his apartment above it, and waved a hand at the women before closing it.

"Isn't he charming?" said Liliane, nudging Amanda and waiting for an expression of approval. Amanda blushed.

"He certainly is."

"So, are you going to see him again?"

"I don't know, maybe... Liliane, enlighten me about something, please. Why do people keep calling me 'the little Canadian?' I know that I'm short, but I'm not *that* short. Orvilly-sur-Mer is not exactly a village of giants, so why do people keep calling me this way?"

Liliane laughed.

"Oh, don't you worry about this. This is just an expression from here, something that Normans say to anybody, when they are younger than them. So, you can stay 'the little someone' for many people for many years, even after you become an adult."

"But what if you are exceptionally tall? Would people keep calling you 'the little I-don't-know-who?' if you were over 6 feet tall?"

Liliane made a pause of reflection.

"Hmm, good point, I'm not sure about that... It might be the exception to the rule."

The women walked in the dark little streets, barely lighted by a few street lamps here and there. They were laughing as they recounted the amusing events of the evening.

Chapter 39

When Amanda opened the door of her hotel room, she faced a peculiar situation. Bronx was on the top of d'Artagnan's head, his claws firmly gripped on the poor dog's face, covering his eyes. The Great Dane couldn't see anything. D'Artagnan was shaking his head vigorously trying to get rid of Bronx, growling in pain, but the wild cat was clinging onto him as if he were on a rodeo ride, screeching in joy.

"What's going on here?" asked Amanda.

The dog and the cat stopped moving immediately.

This is not how it looks, thought d'Artagnan.

This is exactly how it looks, thought Bronx.

Amanda removed Bronx from d'Artagnan's head. As usual, the cat gesticulated and protested, disapproving of the forced end of the battle. He ran to hide under a chair and looked at Amanda with angry eyes. *Let's make it clear that it's no capitulation. I'll get this stupid dog later.*

"What's wrong with you two? The moment my back is turned, and there you go, you jump at each other! Can't you be nice, for a change?"

D'Artagnan mumbled. *Never gonna happen! I did nothing. This crazy cat jumped on me, out of the blue. He should be in an asylum. Are there asylums for cats? Please say yes!*

The dog desperately waited for a positive answer from Amanda. She stood in the middle of the bedroom, hands in the pockets of her wet raincoat. The water dripped on the floor, forming a puddle around her rubber boots.

Bronx looked at her with disdain. *By the way, you're dripping. Just saying...*

"Staying here isn't good for you. It's too small. We need to move to the castle as soon as possible or you'll kill each other."

Amanda felt something in the right pocket of her raincoat. Something, she was pretty sure, that wasn't there before she left the hotel. Surprised, she pulled a crumpled paper out of her pocket. She smoothed it out. Something was written on it.

If you want to know more about the casino, meet me tomorrow night at the castle. 10:05 p.m. sharp.

Amanda wondered who could've put that paper in her pocket and when? She was pretty sure it wasn't there when she left the room to go to the Village Hall, so it must've been someone who was there.

There were about five hundred people in the hall that night, and as her raincoat had remained on the coat rack the whole evening, anybody could've put this paper in her pocket, at any time. It was impossible to figure out who. The only way to find out was to go to this strange rendezvous. But why 10:05 p.m. instead 10 p.m.? What would these five minutes change?

Amanda removed her clothes to slip into her comfy outfit, a striped sweater and pants she had kept since her years in college, which had turned greyish with time after so many years of laundering. She wondered what Pierre would think if he saw her in such apparel. The sexy baker and the 'grungy little Canadian.' Not sure he would find this image very appealing...

She was walking to the bathroom to brush her teeth when she heard a knock at the door. Who could it be at this time of night? It was quite late. She heard another knock. She rinsed her mouth quickly and walked to the door, followed by d'Artagnan. Amanda stood behind the door.

"Who's this?" she asked.

There was a moment of silence.

"You don't know me. I'm staying in the hotel, in the room beside yours."

Amanda turned to d'Artagnan.

"Oh my god, d'Art, it's that strange man," she whispered.

The dog looked at Amanda, waiting for her to do something. She turned back to the door.

"Uh... What do you want?" she asked. "It's quite late and I'm in my pajamas."

"I just have a question to ask you. Please, open the door."

Scared and unsure what was the right thing to do, Amanda half-opened the door reluctantly. D'Artagnan was just beside her, growling, trying to force his head between the doorframe and Amanda's legs, ready to jump up on the stranger who was standing at the door.

"What do you want?" asked Amanda.

The tall man was still wearing his black coat and hat. He looked down at Amanda with a serious expression, his black eyes staring right into hers.

"Did you follow me tonight?"

No introduction, no 'hello my name is...' But his lack of manners was probably not Amanda's major concern at that moment.

"Me, following you? Is that a joke?" answered Amanda, "No, I didn't. Did *you* follow me?"

"No," answered the man, "but I have some advice to give you: whether you were following me or not, I strongly suggest that you don't poke your nose about my business, and that you don't repeat a word about the conversation I had on the phone earlier to *anybody*. I saw you in the bathroom. You were hiding there, listening to me."

Crap! This man was threatening her because she'd overheard him?

"It could be *dangerous*," he continued, stressing the last word, getting closer to the door. He sneaked a glance at her room.

"Are you threatening me?"

"I'm just warning you. Good night."

The man walked down the corridor, and went into his room. Amanda closed her door and sat on her bed. Her heart was beating fast.

D'Artagnan put his head on her lap, giving her the sweetest look. *Guess what I'm going to ask you?*

"Let me guess. I've just been threatened by a dangerous stranger, but you, you want food?"

Bingo! D'Artagnan happily wagged his tail.

Chapter 40

A woman Amanda had never seen before placed mini-cakes and mini-pies on a silver plate with carved handles delicately. She put a lot of care into creating a harmonious arrangement, alternating the shapes and the colors of the pastries. Then she pulled out another tray of hot pastries from a ceramic oven.

Odd, thought Amanda. What was this woman doing in the kitchen castle? How did she get in? And why is she wearing this long brown skirt and a bonnet on her head?

A man wearing a black and white suit, a white cloth over one of his forearms, stepped down into the kitchen.

"Hurry up, we'll bring the cake in a few minutes."

"It's coming, it's coming!" answered the woman, visibly irritated to be rushed. The man left.

A kettle whistled on the cooktop. The woman ran to a cupboard and took out several teacups and saucers that she placed on another silver tray.

She removed the steaming kettle from the cooktop, holding the handle with a rag. She poured the tea into the cups. Then she stopped and looked at the last empty cup on the tray, hesitating.

Why did she stop?

The woman looked in the cupboard on her right, the one from which she had taken the cups. She put the kettle on the table and opened the cupboard. She stood up on the tip of her toes, extending her arm to reach a hidden box placed behind some dishes, on the top shelf. She opened it, looked inside, and looked at the empty teacup on the tray. She opened a drawer, took a teaspoon, and walked back to the tray. She plunged the teaspoon in the box and scooped a spoonful of tiny white flowers that she dropped in the empty cup. She took the kettle and poured tea into it. Her hand was shaking.

The servant in black and white was back.

"Is it ready? I have to take these trays now."

The woman nodded, and the man left with the trays.

As he walked by Amanda, she noticed that the teacup into which the woman had put the white flowers bore the initials M.D.O., written in gold.

She had seen this cup before. Hadn't she?

The woman walked slowly toward Amanda, wiping her hands with a washcloth, and stopped in front of her.

"I'm asking you again. What the hell are you doing in my kitchen?"

❖

Amanda walked along Brigadier Street, still disoriented by the bad dream she had had the previous night. She also wondered if the whole population of Orvilly had deserted the village. Where were all the people? There wasn't a soul in the streets, not even a cat on the sidewalks. Not a sound.

She was surprised and relieved when she saw the bakery open. The little bell rang when she pushed in the door to step into the blue store. Amanda stood alone for a few seconds in front of the displays, admiring the perfectly aligned rows of cakes and pastries inside the glass counters. The colorful and aromatic temptations were an invitation to sin.

"Good morning, Amanda. It's nice to see you again." Pierre arrived from the back room and stood behind the counter, crossing his arms over his chest. The sleeves of his white shirt were rolled up, showing his strong biceps.

Nice, thought Amanda. Apparently making bread and cakes helped to build up muscle.

Pierre smiled when he noticed what she was looking at. She blushed, feeling embarrassed to be so transparent.

"What can I do for you, Amanda?"

"May I have four apple turnovers, please."

"Sure. Would you like them in a box or in a bag?"

"In a box, please."

Pierre took some tongs to grab the half-moon shaped golden pastries and put them in a white box. He sealed the box with a silver sticker, and wrapped it up with a blue string in a fancy bow. Amanda smiled. The man was muscular, and yet quite delicate with his hands.

"Anything else?" asked Pierre.

"Yes. The whole store, please," said Amanda.

They laughed.

"I'm surprised to see that you're open today. All the stores are closed. It's dead outside. What's going on?"

"Nothing," answered Pierre, "it's just Sunday. Nothing happens in cities, and even less in villages, on Sundays in France. Everything is closed, except for bakeries. French people like their baguette!"

"I see. But you never close, then?"

"Yes, I close on Mondays."

"Why is that? French people need baguettes on Sundays, but they don't need any on Mondays?"

Pierre chuckled.

"No, they do. But if they really need bread on Monday, they can go to the grocery store to buy some."

"I see... quite different from Canada. Our stores are open all week long. I guess that buying bread or cakes requires some planning here."

"You can say so. Are you going to share these turnovers with d'Artagnan and Bronx?"

"No, it's not for them, but for someone from Bellevue House."

"Oh, did you finally make friends with Germaine Parmentier?" asked Pierre, doing a funny face.

"Certainly not. I'm going to visit a man there, Louis Lamour. He writes for the Gazette. Maybe you know him?"

Pierre laughed.

"So, he got you already? Damn, this man is old but quick."

"What do you mean?"

"Louis Lamour has the reputation of being the 'Don Juan' of Bellevue House. A lot of ladies there run after him. He always manages to get what he loves the most: apple turnovers and beautiful women. Today, he'll have both. What did he do to deserve such a privilege?"

Amanda blushed and mumbled something. Could an intelligible sentence come out of her mouth?

"Oh, he just agreed to answer a few questions about an article he wrote in the Gazette, to help me with my investigation. In exchange, he asked for turnovers."

"Ah, I see... He practices extortion now to get what he wants."

Amanda giggled.

"If it makes the old man happy, why not," she said. "Well, I have to go now. Thank you, Pierre, have a good day."

Amanda took the box with the turnovers from the counter and walked to the door.

"Amanda?" said Pierre.

Amanda turned around.

"I'm aware that Louis Lamour is way more attractive than I am, but would you accept an invitation for dinner?"

Was there another word for 'blushing' when someone is boiling so much inside that they look as red as a lobster outside?

After a few seconds of silence that felt like ten minutes, Amanda remembered that she had to answer the question.

"Sure. When?"

"What about this Saturday evening? Would that work for you?"

"Sure. Where?"

Gosh! She knew other words than 'sure.'

"At my place, upstairs. We could go to The Old Calvados, but this is the only restaurant in the village, and I'd rather not give people an opportunity to gossip. Do you like Italian food?"

"I love food."

Another brilliant answer...

Pierre laughed.

"Wonderful. Then have a good week, and I'll see you on Saturday for a dinner... with food."

Chapter 41

Amanda arrived at Bellevue House walking on a cloud, bearing an ecstatic grin on her face. She stood in front of the elevator, waiting for the doors to open, but hadn't even pushed the button.

"Madam," said the employee at the desk, "if you're here to visit Mr. Lamour, he's in the dining room, on your left."

"Thank you. How did you know I was here for Mr. Lamour?"

The woman shrugged. "Because you're carrying a box of pastries."

"Ah, I see... The turnovers gave me away."

Amanda walked to the dining room where most of the tables were full. The residents were talking loudly and had just finished their lunch, and were enjoying coffee and dessert. Amanda scanned the room and saw Louis Lamour sitting at a table at the far end. The old man smiled like a child when he saw her walking toward him, carrying a little white box.

"You didn't forget! Good. Sit down," said Lamour.

"Oh, I just came to bring you these," answered Amanda, "I don't want to bother you."

"You don't bother me. I'm bored to death and I'm trying to avoid talking to this one on my left." He gave a sidelong glance at a woman sitting beside him and tapped his hand on an empty chair to invite Amanda to sit down. The elderly woman was all smile, desperately waiting for any hint of interest from Louis Lamour.

"Why don't you want to talk to this lady?" whispered Amanda. "She looks nice."

"She's old, boring and deaf. That's why you don't need to whisper."

The man wasn't afraid of being blunt.

"No offense, Louis, but there are a lot of people like this, here. Including you."

"Me? Not at all! I hear perfectly well, and I'm not boring. Let's see those apple turnovers."

Amanda cut the string and opened the box. Louis's eyes opened wide.

"Wonderful! Have one with me." The man waved at a waitress with a coffee pot in her hands who stood a few tables away from them. She walked toward them. "This lovely woman would like a coffee. Could you pour her some, please, sweetheart?" asked Louis.

The waitress smiled as she poured the beverage into an empty cup on the table. "I see that you have made a new conquest, Mr. Lamour. There's no stopping you."

The old man shrugged and boasted. "What do you want? I'm irresistible."

Amanda and the waitress laughed.

"Lucky you. Well, I'll let you enjoy your date and go back to work then." The waitress winked at them and walked away.

Louis took a turnover in his shaking hands and opened his mouth wide, way before the pastry arrived at destination. He bit into the delicacy, closing his eyes to better savor the moment. "I'm in Heaven. Best turnovers ever!" said Louis, chewing his pastry. "So, tell me, did you learn more about this man in the picture?"

"No, unfortunately, I didn't," said Amanda, disappointed.

Louis Lamour gave her a quick glance of disdain. "You wouldn't make a very good journalist."

Should she take back the box with the three remaining turnovers? Amanda refrained from doing so. Maybe being abrupt was a quality that came with age. "I don't know who this man is *yet*," she stressed the last word, "but I had an unpleasant encounter with him. He knocked at my door last night, threatened me, and ordered me to mind my own business. So, at least, I know that I'm on the right track. And I have a meeting with someone tonight at the castle who's supposed to give me some information."

Louis stopped eating. He looked at Amanda, intrigued. Sadness shaded his eyes. "But, there's nobody left at the castle."

"No. I mean that I'll meet this person somewhere outside, by the castle... Louis, I'm the new owner of the castle, you knew that, right?"

The old man put his half-eaten turnover on the table and froze. "You... you bought the castle?"

Amanda wondered why this news suddenly affected the man. "No, I didn't buy it. I inherited it. What's wrong?"

"So, you knew Toinette?"

"No, unfortunately I never had the chance to meet her. Did you know her?"

A tear formed at the corner of Louis's eye.

"Yes," he whispered, "I knew her very well."

"Was she a friend of yours?"

"We were more than friends. We were lovers."

Amanda was stunned. "You were *lovers*?" said Amanda out loud.

"Shush! Not so loud, people will hear you. The non-deaf ones, I mean. There are some wagging tongues here who love gossiping."

"You and Toinette were *lovers?*" whispered Amanda, still flabbergasted.

"Yes. What's so incredible about that?"

"Nothing... it's just that... I wasn't expecting this. So, you knew Toinette very well?"

"Toinette had been a friend of mine for many years, and the last year before she passed, we became lovers."

Amanda frowned.

"Yes, old people make love too, you know," said the man.

"All right, yes... so you know many things about Toinette and the castle then?"

"I know some things, yes."

"What do you know?"

"Well, let's see… I know about the ghosts." Louis took back his half turnover and kept working on it.

"The ghosts?"

"Yes. Why do you repeat everything I say? Are you deaf too?"

"No, no... tell me about the ghosts, please."

"I can tell you about them. But if I tell you, you'll just think that I'm an old crazy man who's making up stories."

"No, Louis, I promise I won't. In fact, I think that I've seen a ghost there."

Louis turned his head to Amanda with high interest. "Which one?"

Amanda froze.

"'Which one?' What do you mean 'which one?' Is there more than one?"

"Oh yes! So, which one did you see?"

Amanda was slack-jawed.

"Uh... I saw the one in the kitchen."

"Which one in the kitchen?"

Amanda was horrified.

"You mean that there is more than one ghost, *just* in the kitchen?"

"Yes. I just told you, there are a lot of ghosts in this castle! So, which one? Did you see it well?"

"I saw the shape of a woman, I believe, hiding in a corner... Strangely enough, I think I saw her in my dream last night. She wore a long brown skirt, a white shirt and a cap. She must've been a cook there."

"Ah, yeah, that one. She's the nastiest one."

Amanda's throat tightened. "What do you mean by 'nasty?'"

"She yells at people to frighten them so they get out of the kitchen. She displaces dishes and cutlery or even makes them disappear. She locks people in the basement. She still thinks that it's her kitchen. Let's say that she's quite 'territorial.'" Louis had barely finished his first turnover when his hand was already snatching a second one. He took the pastry from the box without hesitation.

"So, she used to work in the castle?"

"Yes. During the nineteenth century."

"The nineteenth century?"

"And you repeat again what I just said! It's getting old, you know... Yes, nineteenth century. I don't know if you've noticed, but nowadays people don't dress the way she does to cook."

"So, if you saw her, Toinette saw her too?"

"Oh yes. Even though Toinette was used to her, she avoided interacting with the cook because she was a real pain in the ass. So Toinette barely used the kitchen after her last employee left. The employee had had enough dealing with this crazy ghost cook."

This explained the piles of empty cans that were found in a bin behind the castle after Toinette died.

"Has she done more than frighten people or displace things?" asked Amanda.

"What do you mean?"

"Has this ghost... killed people?"

"How could a ghost kill someone? You say silly things." They were having a conversation about a ghost, and yet, Amanda was the one saying silly things? "But in her time, she did kill someone though. I think she poisoned the one who's portrait is in the hall, above the chimney. I forgot her name."

"You mean Mélie? She poisoned Mélie d'Orvilly?"

"Yes, that one."

"Why did she do that?"

"I don't know everything about this family! They've been here for centuries. Too many stories."

"All right. But, by any chance, do you know this ghost's name? Or this woman's, shall I say?"

Louis Lamour pondered for a moment.

"Jeannette. I think Toinette told me her name was Jeannette."

"What is she so angry about?"

"Old stories, things that happened in the castle. I told you, I don't know much about all that. I never investigated this. Never had the time nor the desire to do so. Had enough work with my articles for the Gazette." Louis was still eating. The man's stomach had no end.

"So, you said 'them.' What about the *other* ghosts?"

"Oh my God, there's tons of ghosts there! It would be too long to talk about them." Amanda's face turned white. She took a quick sip of coffee.

Louis Lamour was amused. He waved a hand in the air to show that he didn't care. "Don't worry, they're not all nasty like the cook."

Not 'all?' Speaking of 'nasty,' something bad was coming their way, and it wasn't a ghost. A group of women walked toward Louis's table and, lo and behold, Germaine Parmentier was one of them.

"Oh no, are you kidding me?" said Amanda, "Not her again!"

The women were getting closer. Amanda panicked, she had to do something. She didn't want another unpleasant meeting with that awful woman so she pushed her spoon on purpose to drop it on the floor, and dived under the table, pretending to look for it.

"What are you doing?" asked Louis, looking under the table.

"Shush!" whispered Amanda.

"Just grab the damn spoon over there. It's not so difficult. What's wrong with you?"

Unfortunately, the group of women stopped at Louis's table.

"Good afternoon, Louis."

Amanda recognized Germaine's voice.

"I see that you have a visitor today?" The woman pointed at the cup of coffee and the empty seat beside the man.

"Yes," answered Louis.

"Ah. A nice family visit, I suppose?" asked Germaine. The woman sounded extremely agreeable. Did she have a personality disorder?

"No. I forgot her name. But she brought me apple turnovers."

The woman noticed a foot under the table. "What is this person doing under the table?"

"Grabbing a spoon," answered Louis.

Parmentier lifted the salmon table cloth and found Amanda. "You again!" said Germaine Parmentier. "You're everywhere I go! It's unbearable! Are you following me?"

Amanda left her hideout, brushed off some dust on her pants, and sat back on her chair.

"It's a pleasure to see you again Mrs. Parmentier. Why would I want to follow you?"

"Oh, don't be sarcastic or play the innocent with me. I'm not a fool."

"You know each other?" asked Louis Lamour.

"Yes," said Parmentier, "unfortunately we do. She's a sneaky little pest. Be careful Louis, she steals things from people."

"No, that's not true!" protested Amanda.

"You're here to annoy and rob old people, I know it," continued the woman with a hostile tone. "I'm going to report you to management. I've had enough of you!"

Germaine Parmentier walked away with a firm step, followed by her two friends who sent looks of disgust at Amanda.

"You pissed off Parmentier?" asked Louis, amused.

"It was just a succession of unfortunate misunderstandings," explained Amanda.

"I like you better now!" said Louis with a grin.

Amanda blinked. The turnovers hadn't make her likeable enough?

Chapter 42

D'Artagnan pulled on his leash. *No way I'm going outside. Have you seen the weather? You know how much I hate rain!*

"Come on d'Art! This is just a little teeny-weeny rain. It won't hurt you."

Easy for you to say. You have clothes on! The dog sat on his butt with the firm intention of staying in the room.

Amanda kneeled in front of him.

"D'Artagnan, be a good dog. I don't want to go to the castle alone. Please, please, please, come with me. I'll give you a big piece of fresh meat once we're back to the hotel."

Ah, now you're talking. Let's go! The Great Dane pulled on his leash and walked off, forcing Amanda to move forward. She had to trot behind him to keep his pace.

"Not so fast!" protested Amanda.

The dog didn't slow down. *Ah, now you complain? This is what you wanted, so keep up!*

It was 10:04 p.m. and pitch-dark when Amanda and d'Artagnan arrived at the Domaine d'Orvilly. The castle had this gloomy veil again, giving Amanda chills. "How come this castle looks so lovely by day, but so terrifying by night?" she said.

D'Artagnan was on his guard, walking slowly. He mumbled. *What the heck are we doing here at this time of night? What an idea. I don't like it.*

They walked around the outside of the castle, Amanda lighting their way with a flashlight, but they didn't see anybody. Where was this mysterious messenger?

The dog stopped and growled.

"What, d'Artagnan? What is it?"

"Pssst!" said someone.

D'Artagnan barked. Amanda turned around.

"Pssst! Just behind you."

The dog barked again. Amanda turned the other way.

"In the corner, over here," whispered the same voice.

Someone was hiding behind the recess of a pillar. Amanda got closer, but d'Artagnan stopped walking and growled.

"Uh, could you ask your dog to calm down, please? I'm scared of dogs."

"Sure." Amanda patted d'Artagnan to calm him down. "Shush d'Art, all is fine. Stay quiet now."

The Great Dane decreased his growling, but didn't want to remain silent.

"I said quiet."

D'Artagnan mumbled and went quiet.

"I'm glad you're here and on time," said the stranger. "I didn't want to wait too long."

A person with a large hat and a beige trench coat was hiding behind the recess, showing only half their body. A handkerchief covered their mouth to muffle their voice. Was it a man or a woman?

"Why did you want to meet at 10:05 p.m. ?" asked Amanda. "Why not 10 p.m.?"

"Because my preferred show on TV ends at 10 p.m. so I couldn't make it for 10 sharp."

"Ah. I see."

"You're alone?"

"Yes. Well, with my dog, obviously."

"Good. You must understand that I'm taking a huge risk by meeting you tonight. I need to be sure that all this will stay between us. Capisce?"

"Uh, yes, capisce. No word to anybody, I swear. So, what did you want to tell me?"

"I'm not going to tell you anything."

"Hmm... OK. So why are we here?"

"I'm going to give you something. But you must be very careful. Once I give it to you, you're responsible for it. I'll always deny that I gave it to you."

Amanda frowned. "I don't even know who you are."

"Exactly. You don't know and you'll never know."

"OK. Good. So, what is it?"

"Wait a minute, not so fast."

The stranger lifted the brim of their hat a bit and furtively looked around. "I want to make sure there's nobody else here watching us."

Amanda chuckled. "I can assure you that there isn't. It's Sunday, past ten at night, it's dark, cold, and rainy. Believe me, nobody wants to be here now."

So why are we here? wondered d'Artagnan, looking at Amanda with a desperate look meaning 'let's go home.'

"All right. I'm going to give you something of *extreme* importance. You'll have to keep it securely because I have no copy of this. Once it's in your hands, it's gone. Capisce?"

"Yes, yes, capisce... So, what is it?"

With gloved hands, the person reached for a notebook in a plastic grocery bag and handed it to Amanda. She took it, but the stranger didn't let it go.

"Remember. Not a word to anybody, and you never saw me, capi—"

"Yes, yes, capisce. Got it. Thanks."

The person released the book. "That's it. You're on your own now."

The person ran away... and came back.

"I forgot to tell you: the monkey is the million."

"The monkey is the mil—what?" repeated Amanda, puzzled.

The stranger ran away again... and came back again.

"What now?" asked Amanda, confused.

"It's just that my car is parked the other way. Good night."

Amanda watched the stranger running away in the dark.

"'The monkey is the million?'" she looked at d'Artagnan. "What the heck does that mean?"

Don't look at me! How would I know? Are you telling me that we came here at night, in the cold and the rain, so that a crazy stranger gives you a notebook about a monkey!? Seriously?

The dog raised bewildered eyes at Amanda, wondering how people could be so stupid sometimes...

Chapter 43

"The monkey is the million? What the hell does that mean?" asked Kate on the phone.

Amanda was sitting at the little desk in her hotel room, turning the pages of the notebook the stranger had given her.

D'Artagnan was enjoying his promised fresh piece of meat, shamelessly making inelegant noise while chewing, mouth wide open.

Bronx was sitting on a chair in front of him, observing him with disgust. *Dogs! No manners. How can she prefer this beggar to me?*

"I have no clue," said Amanda, "this is what I'm trying to figure out. Looking at the pages, it makes me think of a child's notebook, you know, the ones they make in kindergarten where they put their stickers and draw or write down something about the activities they did during the day in class. I wonder if this person made a mistake and gave me their kid's notebook instead of the right one? I wouldn't be surprised. This person didn't sound very bright."

"Don't jump to conclusions so fast. Is there a name written somewhere on the notebook?"

Amanda perused the document carefully. "No."

"Does it look organized and clean or do you have scribbles here and there?"

"No, it looks organized and clean. No scribbles at all. It's just all these stickers."

"Then it's not a kid's. Believe me, I've got three. If there's not one scribble or a crooked name proudly written on it, it doesn't belong to a kid. Those stickers must be some sort of code. What kind of stickers do you have?"

Amanda reviewed the pages again. "Hmm... I have several stickers of the same banana, several stickers of the same truck, several stickers of the same pencil, and several stickers of the French flag."

"Hmm... What about the monkey then? Do you have a sticker of a monkey somewhere?"

Amanda quickly flipped the notebook's pages.

"Good question... I don't see any. The rest is only blank pages."

"Well, I'm afraid that I can't help you with this now because we're going to the park and the kids are getting impatient. I'll talk to you later."

"All right. Bye for now."

Amanda lay on the bed and kept studying the notebook. She took a notepad and a pen from her nightstand and began to write.

"All right guys. Let's sum up what we have so far," she said to d'Art and Bronx. "We have a victim, Martin Plouque, who was poisoned with a deadly cocktail of pesticides at a construction site." Amanda was waving her hand holding the pen in the air. The pets' eyes were following the moving pen. "This victim was a bad guy, hated by the whole village, and who had the bad habit of blackmailing people. Then, we have some people running the city their own way—the mayor, Desplanques, and Barbon, the construction guy—you follow me?"

D'Artagnan wiped his tongue over his nose, and Bronx closed his eyes.

"OK, let's say you follow. And we have the architect, Montel who hates Barbon because she holds him responsible for the death of her son. And then, we have the casino project. Ah, and I mustn't forget," Amanda whispered, "we have a mysterious guest in this hotel who told me to stay out of this 'I-don't-know-what-yet,' and now I have a notebook with funny stickers. I don't know about you, guys, but it's time that I put all these things together because I'm fed up with living in this room with the two of you. No offense, but we need space."

Bronx opened one eye. *You mean that I'm the one who's fed up living with the two of you. This room is perfect for me. You can leave anytime.*

D'Artagnan looked at Amanda with an optimistic look, mouth opened and tongue out. *I have faith in you. By any chance, do you have another piece of this yummy meat?*

Chapter 44

Beautiful rays of sunshine flooded in Amanda's bedroom that Monday morning. But what really awakened her was her stuffy nose and repetitive cough. Normandy' humid weather had finally gotten to her lungs.

Within a few minutes, Amanda emptied half the tissues in the box on the nightstand. She sat on the bed, moaning and sneezing. D'Artagnan put an empathetic paw on her thigh. *'Told you not to go out last night. You didn't listen to me...*

Bronx was sound asleep near one of the windows, lying on his back, legs up, basking in the sun like a king.

Amanda made the effort to stand on her feet, but felt her head spinning. She held onto the door frame.

Kept warm in her robe, she walked downstairs, hoping Régine would have some hot herb tea to offer her. She found her at a table in the dining room, scratching off an instant lottery game.

"Dammit! Another 5 Euros lost," complained Régine. "Oh my, look at you!" she exclaimed when she saw Amanda. "Sit down, honey. I'll get you something." Régine walked to the old Norman cabinet, all excited.

"Oh nooo..." whispered Amanda.

Régine opened the creaking door, removed several bottles of Calvados from the cabinet, and displayed them proudly on top of it, as if they were part of a precious collection. She put her hands on her hips, going through a self-debate. Which one would best cure a cold? After a few seconds, she reached a verdict and picked a bottle. "This one! It's going to cure you in no time."

Régine removed the screw top of the bottle, took a large empty glass and filled it to the top with the copper-brown liquid. She brought the glass to Amanda who was half awake at the table. Régine put the glass down on the table with a firm hand. "Here you go. Drink this. Only the good old remedies work."

"Régine, I don't think this is a good idea. I'm not used to drink. I'll be drunk and sick if I swallow this." Amanda sneezed and blew her red nose in a tissue. It felt like she had done this a hundred times since she had woken up.

"Who cares? You're sick, you talk through your nose, and you already look drunk. Nobody will see the difference."

Good point, thought Amanda. She took the glass, looked at the liquid with an ounce of doubt, and raised her eyes on Régine. "It really works?"

"Of course, it works! Go ahead."

And Amanda swallowed the large glass of Calvados... in one shot. Her face turned red. She put down the empty glass on the table, hitting it loudly, and yelled.

"Oh my God! That's awful! It burns!"

"Of course it burns! Why did you swallow it all in one shot? I never told you to drink it all in one shot! That's crazy."

"You tell me this now?" complained Amanda, "Oh... now I feel dizzy and my stomach hurts..."

"That's good. It's gonna kill the bug."

"It's gonna kill me too."

"I'll prepare you some toasts and coffee. You'd better not have an empty stomach after drinking this."

As Régine left the room, Titi trotter over, holding something in his mouth. He stopped to look at Amanda with defiance.

"Today, I look as ugly as you, Titi. No, wait. Uglier than you... What do you have in your mouth?" She leaned toward the dog. What seemed to be a business card was stuck in Titi's crooked teeth. "Where did you get that? Don't eat it," said Amanda. "Oh, wait..."

There was a picture of someone on the business card, and Amanda knew this face. She recognized the mysterious client staying in the hotel. She had to get this card, not an easy task.

"Titi, be nice," said Amanda with a soft voice, "come here and give me the card, please."

The tiny dog with the green 'rooster comb' frowned and growled. Amanda directed her hand toward him cautiously. "You're a good dog, Titi. Come on, give me the card."

The dog barked and the card fell on the floor. Amanda seized it quickly. The deceived dog tried to bite her hand.

"Titi! No biting! You're a bad dog. Go to your pillow, now," Régine put a platter in front of Amanda, and pointed a threatening finger at Titi. "I'm so sorry, Amanda. Titi always has a bad temper with customers. I suspect he has an issue with Paul and I running this hotel. Did he hurt you?"

Amanda quickly shoved the business card in the pocket of her robe.

"No worries, Régine, I'm fine."

"Good. Now try my homemade apple jelly on this salted buttered toast, and have some coffee. You'll feel better soon."

Régine had spread half an inch of butter and a generous layer of jelly on the toasts. Amanda felt nauseous. After all, Normandy would not be Normandy without its rich butter and cream, right? As she didn't want to be rude to Régine who was so kind to her, Amanda closed her eyes and bit slowly in the first slice, feeling relieved that, for once, food didn't taste of anything. She chewed and forced a smile. Régine smiled back proudly.

"Régine, what do you know about this guest staying in the room next to mine. Have you seen him before?"

"Mister Durant? No, not as far as I can remember."

"That's his name, Durant?"

"Yes, Marc Durant. Why do you ask? Is there a problem with him?"

"Oh no, not at all. He looks familiar and I thought I knew him from somewhere, but I must be wrong."

The phone at the reception desk rang.

"Excuse me one minute," said Régine. She walked away to the desk.

While masticating her chunky toast, Amanda had a look at Régine's instant lottery game left on the table. There were five slot machines that had to be scratched off to reveal various hidden symbols of different values. The symbols were fruits, and the strawberry symbol had the highest value. So, the more strawberries were uncovered, the higher the price. Unfortunately, Régine's game had apples and grapes only, which had won her nothing.

Régine came back in the dining-room and pointed at the game with a bitter face. "Yeah, see, I earned peanuts."

And although her brain was foggy, when Régine said the word 'peanuts,' Amanda finally understood something.

Chapter 45

*P*atrick Leroy
A. F. I. Department
French National Lottery

Wrapped up warmly in bed with two additional blankets Régine had given her, Amanda read the business card several times. No doubt, this picture was of the mysterious guest.

"A.F.I.? What does that mean? So... my mysterious neighbor is lying, registered in the hotel as Marc Durant whereas his real name is Patrick Leroy... And, surprise, he works for the French National lottery. Certainly not a coincidence. Why does he need to lie about his identity? What do you think, guys?"

D'Artagnan's attention was absorbed by a cartoon playing on TV. The dog's ears perked up as he followed the fast action on the screen.

Bronx woke up slowly, stretched his legs, and yawned loudly without shame. *What time is it?*

"I only see two possibilities," continued Amanda. "Patrick Leroy is either here because he was involved in some bad business related to the casino project— maybe he and Martin Plouque knew each other and had made some deal together?—or, maybe, he needs to hide his identity for another reason. The French National lottery might have sent him here on purpose? Either way, it's related to the casino project for sure."

D'Artagnan stood up and barked at the television. A character from the cartoon—a cat—was harassing a dog and chasing him away. This re-enactment of his actual life was too disturbing for the dog. *Damn cats! They're all the same!*

Bronx smiled. *That's called good reality TV.*

"D'Artagnan, shush! Behave please," said Amanda.

The dog stopped barking and made a weird noise that sounded like a descending growl. He sat down, eyes fixed on the television screen, hoping that justice would prevail.

Amanda flipped again the pages of the notebook. There were several rows of stickers on several pages. Each row started with one truck sticker, or one flag sticker, or one pen sticker. For the first time, Amanda noticed something else. The same tiny signature at the end of each row. But she couldn't read it. She could only recognize the first letters of the first and last names: J.P.

"Hmm... J.P. Who's J.P.?"

Amanda reviewed all the names of the people she knew in Orvilly-Sur-Mer and wrote them down on a paper.

"Wait a minute..." said Amanda, "this could be the notary's initials, Jean Perrier. Has Jean Perrier anything to do with all this?"

A white page fell from the notebook. Amanda picked it up. It was a drawing, the type that you discover once you connect dots. Someone had started it, but there were just a few lines on the paper, not enough to see the final picture. Amanda took her pen and connected the remaining dots. Her cell phone rang. It was Kate. She answered with one hand, and kept connecting the dots with the other. Then, finally, the full picture appeared.

"Of course! Of course!" exclaimed Amanda.

"Of course, *what*?" asked Kate. "Your voice sounds weird. Do you have a cold?"

"Kate, I think I found it!"

"Found what?"

"The monkey!"

"Which monkey?"

"You know, the monkey mentioned by the stranger I met at the castle the other night."

"Oh yes, that monkey. So, where was it?"

"Hidden in the notebook. And what does a monkey love?

"Uh… bananas?"

"Exactly, Kate, bananas. But most importantly, now the question is: how much is a banana worth?"

"Uh… what?"

Chapter 46

The first thing Amanda did on Tuesday morning was to pay an unexpected visit to Mr. Perrier in his office.

Titillated and intrigued by Amanda's request to talk to Mr. Perrier immediately, Gisèle Poisson tried to gather some information from her, without success.

"This is a very personal matter and it's urgent. It's all I can say, Mrs. Poisson," answered Amanda to put off the nosy assistant.

Mr. Perrier had just arrived in his office. He was drinking his morning coffee, reading through his emails. He invited Amanda in, and as soon as the door was closed, Gisèle Poisson leaned and glued her ear to it. The door reopened. The assistant staggered and blushed to be caught red-handed. She walked back to her desk quickly.

"No listening to my conversations, Gisèle. Please, prepare the files for this morning's appointments and bring them to me later. Thank you." The notary closed the door.

Amanda left Mr. Perrier's office fifteen minutes later, walking hastily to the front door, forgetting to say goodbye to the assistant.

Gisèle Poisson felt more bothered with the fact that she knew nothing about what happened in the meeting, than being ignored by Amanda. If the biggest gossip in the village couldn't feed on the latest news, she couldn't spread rumors. What a shame.

Then Amanda walked to Bellevue House, jumped in the elevator, exited on the third floor, and knocked on the door of room 347. Louis Lamour opened the door, very surprised to see Amanda unannounced.

"They let you in downstairs? Without even bringing me pastries?"

"Forget about the pastries for now, Louis," said Amanda. "I'll offer you apple turnovers *for life* if you'd be willing to do something for me."

The man's face lit up. "Name it!"

"Can you forget about your ethics as a journalist for one day?" she asked.

Louis frowned and looked dubious.

"Remember, I just said the words 'apple turnovers *for life*,'" insisted Amanda.

The man imagined a pile of white boxes filled with his favorite pastries. He gave up on his principles easily.

"OK, fine. What do I have to do?"

"Can I come in for a few minutes? All this must stay between us."

Louis let Amanda in. When she left his room half an hour later, she crossed the path of Mrs. Parmentier in the corridor. Amanda stopped the woman before she even opened her mouth.

"No, Mrs. Parmentier, I'm not here to steal from you or anybody. In fact, let me tell you something: you're the most unpleasant elderly lady I've ever met. You're rude, inconsiderate, and you don't even notice that everybody hates you. To put it simply: you're popular, but not in a good way. If I were you, I'd change my attitude because the senior years that you have left might feel very lonely if you don't. Have a good day, Mrs. Parmentier."

And Amanda walked back to the elevator, leaving the woman standing still in the corridor, speechless. Mouth open, flabbergasted, Germaine Parmentier watched the rude Canadian walk away.

Another lady passed by Amanda and winked at her. "Kudos for shutting her trap good!" she whispered. Amanda smiled proudly.

She was on her way to close some more traps, and it was time.

Chapter 47

La Gazette d'Orvilly-sur-Mer

Wednesday, May 2, 2018

The Castle d'Orvilly Without an Heiress!
What Will The Old Estate Become?

By Louis Lamour

Breaking news on this Tuesday evening as we are working on our next edition of The Gazette, forces us to publish this last-minute article: Mr. Jean Perrier, notary of Orvilly-Sur-Mer, has just informed us that a mistake was made when putting together the family-tree of Mrs. Toinette d'Orvilly, which revealed that the Canadian Amanda McBride is *not* related to the family, and therefore, is *not* the heiress of the deceased woman's castle.

The Mayor, Charles Desplanques—who was informed by Mr. Perrier himself of this sudden turn of events—expressed his astonishment when we spoke with him on the phone, as well as his concern regarding the castle's future, falling now under a fateful deadline to be declared public property by the government.

Before Ms. McBride was appointed as the heiress of the Domaine d'Orvilly, the old castle was already at risk to be 'taken over' from Orvillians by the State, to become public property, and thus facing the risk of being destroyed. An alternative solution had been voted for by our citizens last year during a stormy meeting at The Village Hall to keep the castle in the hands of its fellow citizens, with a submission filed to the French National Lottery to turn the castle into a casino, a decision that some villagers had disapproved vehemently at that time.

We tried to reach Ms. McBride to get her reaction on this breaking news as this debate is about to reopen, but without success.

The Mayor has called for an urgent meeting: all Orvillians are invited to gather at The Village Hall, this Friday, May 4, 2018, at 4 p.m. to discuss the future of our famous heritage building.

Will the old castle remain our property and be turned into a casino as it was supposed to be before Ms. McBride was discovered as the heiress? Or will it be taken into the control of the State, with an uncertain future?

The villagers gathered around the bar counter at The Old Calvados couldn't resist debating about the breaking news while the owner, Roger Poutou, was reading out loud the Gazette article to his customers.

A short and bulky man with a thick moustache, wearing a beret, was gulping down one glass of red wine after another, talking and pointing a finger in the air like a 'know-it-all.' "I tell you it's going to be pretty interesting on Friday! I bet you that the mayor and Barbon will push us to vote for the casino project again. Personally, I've had enough of this old castle and the silly stories about it. We need this location to build other things, something useful, like a supermarket, but not a damn casino! Stupid people who want to lose their money in gambling can drive to Paris or even to Monaco if they want, I couldn't care less."

Gérald Gustin, the owner of the local grocery store, turned red. "Well, excuse me sir, but you're just saying that you don't care about my business! I'd go bankrupt if they opened a supermarket there. It'd ruin my business in no time. And I don't think that our villagers want an ugly supermarket in Orvilly. They want the good local products that I sell in my store. I'm sure they'd rather give *me* their money, than to a big store chain. And the castle is on an amazing location. Really, this is what you want? To build an ugly supermarket there, just by the ocean, while we could turn this castle into a museum and make money?"

Someone laughed. "Nobody makes money out of a museum, you fool," said a man. "And by the way, sometimes you sell rotten apples, Gérald."

Gustin gave a cold look to the man. "This is not true! How dare you?"

"OK, OK, calm down people, please," said Roger, "you know what I think? I think that the French

National Lottery could very well refuse the casino project... for now."

An old woman who was knitting, sitting at a table a few feet away from the counter, and drinking a cider from the bottle, pointed a needle at the group of men.

"You're worse than women gossiping, you old farts! I hope that the castle will be saved because it's our history, our identity. If we lose the castle, we lose our tourists too, and you can say goodbye to all our businesses! I agree that turning the place into a museum wouldn't make it financially. But I hate the casino project. Always been against it. It would be the end of our beautiful village. It's too bad that this Canadian woman isn't the heiress. After all, she had the best project of all. I've heard that she wanted to turn the castle into a fancy hotel or something. The only hotel we have in the village is The Little Norman, and during summer, it gets full very fast to the point that Régine and Paul have to refuse guests! So, tourists don't stay here, they go and spend their money elsewhere. And who cares about the ghosts stories? They're good. They attract the tourists. But you, fools, don't get that. You'd better think about all this before the meeting at the Village Hall on Friday because when the moment comes to vote, we'll all have the fate of Orvilly-Sur-Mer in our hands. Remember that."

Sitting in a far back corner, hiding her face in the collar of her raincoat, Amanda was eating a quiche and a salad, delighted to hear that the breaking news had re-ignited the fire about the castle's fate.

Little did The Old Calvados customers know, this was not the only breaking news they were about to hear...

Chapter 48

Orvilly-sur-Mer's Village Hall had never been so full. There was no empty space, and people could barely move, standing tight beside each other like canned sardines.

The mayor was on the stage, waiting for Gérald Gustin to fix an issue with the microphone. The tension was high and the conversations going on created a hubbub that raised in volume by the second. Finally, the microphone was working. Gérald handed it to Charles Desplanques.

"Fellow Orvillians, I need your attention, please," said the mayor, waving his hands in a downward motion. The volume lowered progressively to total silent. We could've heard a pin drop.

"As you all know," continued Desplanques, "unexpected news has forced us to call this urgent meeting. The future of our castle is in jeopardy again, but I believe its fate is in our hands. I want to make sure that we all make the right decision to keep the castle under our control, and make use of it in a way that benefits our community. We have a tight deadline before the estate becomes public property. Therefore, the members of the city council and myself have decided to go ahead with the casino project, an option that had been discussed last year."

Comments roared from the crowd and half of the people in the room booed.

"You don't have the right to make this decision! We have the right to vote!" yelled someone in the crowd. "This casino project is bad! It's going to benefit just a small number of people, but it'll be the end of our quiet village for sure. We don't want gamblers here. That only brings trouble!"

Some people applauded, others whistled in approval, and some booed again.

"I know that it's impossible to make everybody happy with this casino project," answered the mayor. "But it's the only solution that makes sense, and the timing is crucial. We keep the castle and it brings money into our community. Everybody wins."

"This is our history and heritage, mayor," yelled the knitter from the bistro. "How can you take such a revolting decision? If there's no castle, but an ugly casino instead, there's no Orvilly-sur-Mer anymore. We'll become a village like any other around here. The tourists we had coming every summer will stop visiting, and it'll be the end of our economy. And I strongly doubt that we'll ever see a cent from this casino's profits, am I right, people? This is what you tell us now, but it's all lies! Nothing has ever been clear about the profits part!"

"I'm with our mayor on this," said someone else, "what do you want to do with a falling down ruin and stupid ghost stories that only fascinate grungy teenagers looking for a thrill? I find all of you very selfish. You want to keep this castle, but I bet that none of you would donate money or move their little finger to save it! The mayor is right. Let's build a casino, our community needs the business!"

All the villagers started arguing, forgetting about the mayor on the stage. The heat rose in the Hall and the atmosphere became dangerous. People were yelling at each other, some were about to fight, showing threatening fists.

Charles Desplanques yelled into his microphone, asking the villagers to calm down, but the crowd was so loud that nobody could hear him.

Amanda stepped onto the stage and took the microphone from the mayor's hands. He looked surprised to see her there.

"What are you doing here?" he asked.

Amanda ignored him and turned to the crowd. "People, please, listen to me!" yelled Amanda. "The future of the castle is safe and it will bring in money. But not with a casino."

The crowd went silent when they heard the Canadian accent. Hundreds of puzzled eyes stared at Amanda.

"What are you still doing here?" yelled someone. "this is none of your business anymore. Let us discuss this between us, little Canadian."

Some people in the assembly laughed.

"In fact," pursued Amanda, "it's absolutely *my* business. I'm the one who came up with the story you read in the Gazette, announcing that I'm not Toinette d'Orvilly's heiress. I had to tell a lie so that the whole village would come to this special meeting."

Louis Lamour was in the assembly, smiling like a little boy proud of his prank.

Protests rose in the Hall. Desplanques was perplexed.

"What... What are you talking about?" he asked Amanda. "And where is Jean Perrier? This is not what I've been told by our notary, earlier this week."

Jean Perrier stood quietly on the side of the stage, but didn't say anything.

"What the heck is this? We don't need lies!" yelled someone. "We need a solution!"

"This is exactly what I'm about to provide," answered Amanda. "But I'm not the only one telling a big lie, here. Truth is, the mayor himself has been lying to you for a while now."

"Don't you dare call me a liar!" Desplanques frowned and straightened up, sending a threatening look at Amanda.

Despite her petite 5'3 frame, the 'little' Canadian didn't feel intimidated and didn't move an inch. Holding firmly to the microphone in one hand, she pointed an accusing finger at the mayor with the other. "This man here has been lying to you because his plan was to make big profits with the casino project. And you're right, you'd probably receive peanuts for your community. Him pushing for the casino was definitely not an altruistic act, am I right, Mr. Desplanques? And this is why Martin Plouque died."

"You're crazy! Nobody understands what you're talking about," protested the man. "Everybody here knows that my priority as a proud mayor of Orvilly-sur-Mer is to ensure that my village and my citizens are well taken care of. And I've been doing this successfully for over twenty years. And Martin Plouque was a bum anyway, a petty criminal. We all knew things would go very wrong for him, one day or another."

"Yeah, that's true," yelled someone, "for the moment, the only liar in this room is you, Ms. McBride!"

Some people applauded.

"I want to hear more about this," said Régine who stood beside her husband Paul, near the entrance. "I think we should listen to Amanda before dismissing what she has to say. So, what's this all about, Amanda?"

"Martin Plouque was killed because he knew too much," said Amanda.

Some people laughed.

"Yeah, he knew too much and did too much! No big news here!" said someone "Like the mayor said, Martin knew what was coming to him."

"He knew too much about the casino project," replied Amanda. "Especially the fact that the mayor was guaranteed to receive a kickback of a million Euros if the casino project was approved," said Amanda.

This last piece of information left the villagers mute.

"What the heck is this story?" asked someone.

"We need proof!" yelled Barbon who was at the other end of the Hall, standing there with his employees.

"Not only do I have proof, Mr. Barbon," answered Amanda, "but I know that you were part of this deal too!"

This upsetting revelation threw another bomb into the crowd. An old lady turned to a man beside her.

"What is going on?" she asked, "is this a new play?"

"No, Ma'am," answered the man, "but it's becoming very interesting entertainment, for sure."

"You're making serious accusations here, Ms. McBride," said Barbon. "if I were you, I'd be very careful with the next words that leave my mouth."

"You don't scare me either, Mr. Barbon," replied Amanda. "But I'm not done yet. Mrs. Delphine Montel too was part of this deadly plot against Martin Plouque. But not so much for the money. For another reason. A very personal one. Am I right, Mrs. Montel?"

All heads turned to the architect who was standing in the middle of the crowd, looking at Amanda coldly.

"You can say whatever you want, nobody believes you," said the woman. "All this is silly. Why would I want to kill Martin Plouque?"

"Because you think that he was responsible for your son's death a few years ago. Desplanques and Barbon convinced you to put money in the casino project. You agreed to do it, but not only for the financial investment. In exchange, you wanted Martin Plouque dead."

Delphine Montel's face became as white as a sheet. She didn't say a word, staring at Amanda. The room was silent. People were waiting for the architect to deny the accusations. But instead, the woman smiled. With a big smile. A big scary smile.

"Wow... I've never seen this woman smile before," whispered a man beside her. "And frankly, I prefer it when she doesn't."

"Martin Plouque was a bloody fool who cared about nothing and nobody," said Montel. "He took advantage of every single person in this Hall. But what he did to my son was unforgivable. Getting rid of him was the best thing to do. I wish it had been done sooner. I have no regrets."

The crowd was stupefied. Everybody had their eyes and mouth wide open.

"Are you sure this is not a game or something?" asked the same old lady to the man standing beside her. "Uh... I'm afraid not, ma'am," answered the man.

Two police officers standing by the Hall entrance made their way through the crowd to Delphine Montel. People whispered. When the officers reached the architect, the woman showed her wrists willingly, still smiling. The men put her in handcuffs and escorted her to the exit while people stared, in total disbelief.

"So, it looks like we have a murderer who admitted what she did and she just got arrested," said the mayor. "There's nothing more to talk about. Meeting adjourned!"

"Not so fast!" yelled someone, "what about the two of you?"

The villagers divided all their attention between Barbon and Desplanques.

Liliane approached the stage and handed something to Amanda. It was the notebook with the stickers. She opened the notebook and showed it to Desplanques.

"Do you recognize this, Mr. Desplanques?"

Desplanques looked at the notebook with disdain.

"This? I don't even know what it is. But it looks like a child's notebook. What's your point, Ms. McBride?"

Amanda turned to the crowd and waved the notebook above her head.

"And you, Mr. Barbon, "yelled Amanda. "Do you recognize this notebook?"

"I don't write in kids' notebooks, Ms. McBride. I use proper letters and numbers, you know, I'm a grown up."

The assembly laughed.

"Precisely, Mr. Barbon. If you, the mayor, and Mrs. Montel had written in this notebook using proper language and numbers, it would've been too obvious. What you did instead was to create a notebook that looked like a child's one, so that nobody would pay attention to it. But this, what I'm holding in my hands, dear Orvillians, is the proof that the trio Desplanques-Barbon-Montel was putting money together to bribe someone. Someone who would help them to have the casino project approved. Because it was a long shot. You knew that the French National Lottery wouldn't approve the casino project so easily, so you had to convince someone working there to approve the project. Am I right, Mr. Marc Durant? Or should I say Patrick Leroy, your real name on your business card."

Amanda took out of her jeans pocket the business card Titi had found and displayed it in direction of the tall man in a black coat who stood in a corner of the room.

"Very well done, Ms. McBride," said Patrick Leroy. "You could work as a private investigator yourself for the French National Lottery."

"Thank you, Mr. Leroy. And you certainly know what you're talking about because this is exactly why you're here, right? To investigate this bribe for the casino project? It's what these initials on your business card mean: A. F. I. for Accounts and Frauds Investigation."

The tall man looked at the crowd.

"Ms. McBride is right," answered Leroy. "I work for The French National Lottery, and I'm here because there's an open investigation about a bribe related to the casino project here."

The whole crowd exhaled in unison a sound of stupefaction.

"Last year," continued the man, "we noticed unusual numbers in some of our accounts. We understood quickly that an employee was involved in a bad game, so we started to watch him. This employee communicated regularly with your mayor to collect money, money that was put together by the mayor himself, Mr. Barbon and Mrs. Montel. This employee had promised them that the casino project would be approved if they raised a million Euros for him, and they would have in return a guarantee of doubling their 'investment' within the first year, once the casino opened. The notebook that Ms. McBride is holding is the proof that I needed to complete my investigation. The stickers were used as a code between the three of them to keep track of their payments."

All the villagers turned in shock to their mayor.

"What's this children's notebook thing about?" asked the elderly lady to the man. "I don't understand a thing that's going on here. Why are we here?"

"Oh my God!" answered the man, delighted, "What's going on here is pretty awesome, Mrs. Bertrand, it's even better than a play!"

The lady frowned, totally confused.

"But what about Martin's death?" asked someone in the crowd.

"It's pretty simple," said Amanda. "At some point, Martin Plouque, who had the nose for this kind of illegal deal figured out the trio's business, and realized that he himself could make big money out of it. So, he blackmailed them. This is when Desplanques, Barbon and Montel agreed to kill Martin Plouque. While working on the site at the castle, Barbon stole pesticides from the landscaper's truck and made a deadly cocktail that he spread on Martin's slice of apple pie. The apple pie that I had cooked. One bite was enough to kill the man. Barbon tried to pin this murder on the young landscaper, Martin Verroyer."

"That's ridiculous!" protested Barbon. "You have no proof!"

"When I left the castle that day, I noticed that you had a rash on your right arm. Pesticides go through to your skin, Mr. Barbon, even if you wear gloves, and traces can still be on your body for a while. A simple analysis will prove this."

"How could you?" shouted someone at Barbon and Montel, "and I've been voting for you as mayor for twenty years! You filthy criminals!"

Everybody started to yell in the Hall. Four policemen arrested Charles Desplanques and Auguste Barbon, and escorted them to the exit accompanied by the boos of the villagers who were ready to attack them.

Patrick Leroy walked to the stage and shook Amanda's hand. She gave him the notebook.

"Good Job, Amanda," said the man. "But it could've been very dangerous for you. This is why I tried to warn you. This criminal trio was planning to kill you next."

Amanda froze. She had been so absorbed in solving this that she had not envisioned for one minute she might've been the next target of these criminals.

"Well, Inspector McBride," said Liliane with a humorous tone, "what about a good meal and a glass of red wine to celebrate the end of a mystery that you solved brilliantly?"

Liliane and Amanda walked slowly to the exit, surrounded by the crowd. Villagers were thanking 'the little Canadian,' shaking her hands, patting her back. Many people expressed their astonishment for being so gullible about all this.

Joséphine Perrin, the mayor's assistant, walked by Amanda, who stopped her.

"Madam, I believe this belongs to you, right? I found it in front of the castle this morning, when walking my dog." Amanda gave a blue pompom to the assistant. One of the blue pompoms she had noticed on the assistant's shoes when she had visited the mayor's office to request a building permit. "But no worries," whispered Amanda. "Capisce?" She winked.

Joséphine Perrier put the blue pompom in her pocket and rushed to the exit.

"What was that about?" asked Liliane to Amanda.

"Oh, nothing," answered Amanda simply.

"So, what's next?" asked Liliane.

"Next is moving to the castle tomorrow morning and... getting ready for a date with Pierre tomorrow night."

Liliane got all excited when hearing this news and grabbed her friend's shoulders.

"Oh my God! We have so much to do. Have you heard the term 'makeover,' Amanda?"

The little Canadian grimaced.

"Yes. I've heard this word many times coming out of Kate's mouth, my best friend in Victoria."

"Well, I don't know this Kate, but I already love her. Honey, sometimes you gotta do what you gotta do!"

Amanda felt a bit anxious, unsure what these last words would entail. But she knew she had to work on some serious improvement regarding her 'look.' Although her appearance had never been her priority, this time she had very good motivation to consider. And this motivation smelled as good as a warm bread, and probably tasted as sweet as apple pie...

Chapter 49

Amanda was walking in a garden, surrounded by luxurious trees with leaves of a vivid green. She felt peaceful. But as she was walking through the garden, she realized that she could not see anything but these trees. What was behind them? Where was she?

A bird was singing a lovely melody. Amanda raised her head and saw dozens of little birds with multicolored shiny feathers sitting in the trees. Then, the birds and the trees transformed into wallpaper. The same wallpaper that was in Toinette d'Orvilly's bathroom, except it looked brand new.

Amanda heard a woman humming a cheerful tune. A woman in her fifties was sitting on a little stool in front of Amanda. She was looking at her reflection in the mirror of an ornate vanity cabinet, combing her greying hair into a bun, inserting hairpins delicately. When she noticed Amanda in the mirror, standing behind her, she turned and smiled.

"Oh, here you are!"

Amanda was intrigued. She understood she was in Toinette d'Orvilly's private bathroom, but how did she get there? And why was everything in good condition unlike the last time she had visited the bathroom. Who was this woman? Was she—

"Don't you recognize me?" asked the woman.

Amanda hesitated before answering. It seemed that her memory was playing tricks on her. Did she really know this woman? She wasn't sure. She frowned.

"I'm Toinette. Toinette d'Orvilly."

The woman stared at her, smiling, waiting for a reaction from Amanda. But Amanda felt lightheaded. Everything was misty in her mind.

"Welcome to the castle, chérie. You'll love it here. I know that you'll take good care of it."

Toinette turned back to the mirror and applied some pink blush to her cheeks. She moved her hands with the elegance of a ballet dancer.

"Did you know that I'd always dreamed of being a ballet dancer, Amanda?"

Did she read my mind? wondered Amanda.

Toinette giggled.

"You did a great job to save us, Amanda. We're *all* very grateful."

"Who's 'we?'," asked Amanda.

"Don't worry too much about this for now, chérie," said the woman while applying lipstick to her lips, "you'll get used to us. I have two favors to ask you though. May I?"

"Sure? What are they?" asked Amanda.

Toinette sprayed a cloud of subtle flowery perfume on her neck.

"To understand us, you have to unveil the mysteries of Orvilly. The mysteries of our castle and its history."

"Sure... But I don't really understand what you mean."

Which mysteries was Toinette talking about?

"You'll understand. You like reading, don't you?" Amanda nodded. "So, read. There are plenty of books to read in this castle. You're curious and smart, so look around you. Here's my second request: don't be too hard on Jeannette."

"Jeannette, the horrible cook in the kitchen?"

Toinette made a face.

"That's exactly what I mean. Don't be too hard on her. She didn't have an easy life. Will you remember this?"

"I think..." answered Amanda, unsure.

"Good. Now, sorry, but I have to go."

The wallpaper with the birds faded away slowly, and so did Toinette who gave a sweet smile to Amanda, until everything vanished in the air.

Chapter 50

Saturday morning felt like the lick of a giant tongue on Amanda's face. Wait. It *was* one.

Wake up, wake up, wake up. I'm starving! D'Artagnan was cleaning up Amanda's face at the speed of light.

"D'Art, no, stop!"

Amanda sat up in the bed. "Gross!" complained Amanda. "And not a nice way to be awakened."

Yes, but it worked. The dog was looking at Amanda with a big smile on his face.

"Gee, d'Art, don't you ever think about anything else but food?"

Like what? What else is there in life more important than food? The Great Dane was genuinely perplexed.

Like kicking your ass, thought Bronx with an angry morning look, walking fast behind the dog in the direction of the bathroom.

"OK guys, today is *the* big day. We officially move to the castle. Hooray!"

Amanda waited for a reaction of joy and victory from her roommates, but one was standing in front of her, silent, and the other one was doing his business, in the bathroom.

"I love you guys, but sometimes..." Amanda stood up and walked to the cabinet, followed closely by d'Artagnan. She grabbed a big bag. Excited to smell his breakfast, the Great Dane pushed her and tried to put his head in the bag.

"Calm down d'Art. You had some of these yesterday, and the day before, and the day before that, remember? It's not like it's brand new to you."

Amanda poured croquettes into the dog's bowl. D'Artagnan rushed toward it and ate the contents in seconds, as if he had never eaten before in his life. He stopped once the bowl was perfectly clean.

Then the dog licked his chops and looked at Amanda. *So good! Can I have more?*

Bronx quickly ran behind them and jumped on the windowsill.

Bronx came back in the room, looking very proud of himself. *I left you a surprise in the bathroom!* The cat stationed in front of the middle window and started his observation of Brigadier Street.

Amanda walked to the bathroom and stopped at the doorframe, pinching her nose.

"Oh my God! Bronx, what the...? It's really time that we get out of here!"

Ah, ah! Surprise! The cat kept his composure, not the least disturbed by the situation.

D'Artagnan followed Amanda to the bathroom and came back in the bedroom at once. *OMG! Is this for real? Man, this cat's poop, will never get used to it. So gross!*

Bronx furtively looked at d'Artagnan. *Shut up, big legs, you can talk, you and your gigantic sh—*

Amanda's cell phone rang. She picked it up and set it on hands free to start packing up for the move.

"I got your text yesterday," said Kate, "congratulations! I'm so proud of you that you got those idiots arrested."

"Yep, I did! Let me tell you, it was something. At some point, people were starting to fight in the Hall."

"So, what was this notebook with the stickers about then?"

"A record of all the payments the mayor, the construction guy and the architect gave as a bribe to the French National Lottery's employee. It was quite simple, in fact. The truck sticker was for Barbon, the construction guy, the pen sticker was for Montel, the architect, and the French flag was for Desplanques, the Mayor. The banana stickers represented the money. Each banana was worth 10,000 Euros. The mayor's assistant, Joséphine Poirier, collected the payments and put her initials beside each banana when someone made a payment."

"But what about the monkey thing, then?" asked Kate.

"The criminal trio had to reach the bingo, which was represented by the dot-to-dot monkey drawing at the end, in order to obtain the lottery's employee's favor: having the casino project approved by the French National Lottery."

"Holy Moly! That's some expensive bananas. But that's so silly. Why did they choose such a method to track their payments?"

"Well, they didn't want to leave any digital trace of their payments made in cash, but as they didn't trust each other, especially Montel who hated Barbon, they decided that this system wouldn't attract any attention. It would've worked if Joséphine Poirier, the mayor's assistant, hadn't had enough of this. Desplanques had never explained her what all this was about, but she knew that it was bad business. As she had the same initials as the notary, Jean Perrier, I assumed for a while that maybe the notary was in cahoots with the trio too. But when I went to question him and showed him the notebook, he immediately recognized the mayor's assistant's signature. And guess what? She was my secret informant, the one who gave me the notebook. I found one of the blue pompoms from her shoe outside the castle, yesterday. Seeing all this laundered money when you live on an assistant's salary isn't worth taking the risk of going to jail. So she decided to do something."

"Does this mean that this young landscaper who was in jail is free now?"

"Yes! Antoine Verroyer was released yesterday evening, after the meeting at the Village Hall. I feel so sorry for him. The poor guy spent over a week in jail because of them. And he had just started his business. When I told him that I'd hire him again and that I'd give him good references without hesitation, he cried."

"So, the castle renovations can resume?"

"Yes Ma'am! But not with the same company, of course. I've hired a new team from a city nearby. The work will start on Monday. But today, it's a big day for d'Artagnan, Bronx, and I. We're finally moving to the castle!"

Bronx was basking in the sun, curled up, his head buried in his belly. *You two can move away. I stay here.*

I wish! thought d'Artagnan. The dog was very tempted to push the cat out the open window behind him.

"That's great news, Amanda. Aren't you scared about staying in this huge place alone?" asked Kate.

Amanda pondered for a moment, thinking of the ghosts. "Well, if a woman like Toinette d'Orvilly did, so can I." Amanda looked at d'Artagnan and Bronx. She smiled. "And I won't be alone. I'll have some good companions with me. D'Art will protect me. Right, d'Art?"

The dog stood up and looked at Amanda.

Is this about me? What are you saying? Are you talking about me?

Egocentric dummy... thought Bronx who was about to start a nap.

"That's great news Amanda, I'm so happy for you. So, now, let's talk seriously: are you ready for your date? I mean, *really* ready. Did you do some shopping? Book an appointment in a hair salon? Don't forget to do your nails, you—"

"Kate, calm down," said Amanda. "My new friend Liliane is on a mission: she'll accompany me this afternoon for some shopping in the best stores in the area. She told me that I needed a 'makeover.'"

"Oh, Gosh, I don't know this Liliane, but I already love her. OK, now that I know you'll be in good hands, I can go back to my two little devils. Good luck for tonight with Pierre. Don't be scared to bring out the sexy in you, girl!"

Amanda chuckled and hung up. She looked at herself in the mirror of the rustic closet.

"'Bring out the sexy in me,'" she whispered. "I'm not even sure it's in here..."

Chapter 51

Titi was biting d'Artagnan's paws, jumping all around him like a flea to provoke him. The Great Dane wondered what this ridiculous tiny dog was trying to accomplish.

"We're going to miss you Amanda," said Régine, "but it's good to know you won't be too far. Never hesitate to come by and say hi. We'll enjoy a good glass of Calva together."

The woman winked and kissed Amanda on her cheeks four times. Paul walked to Amanda and opened his arms. "Let me give you a good Canadian hug." Paul crushed Amanda's tiny body on his chest. "I'm so proud of you and what you did yesterday at the Village Hall. Always disliked this mayor and his clique. Good riddance of all of them."

"Wait, I prepared something for you." Régine handed a cake pan to Amanda, still warm. The sweet smell of chocolate warmed Amanda's taste buds.

D'Artagnan didn't ignore the scent either and went straight to the pan to have a good look. His eyes rounded up. *Yes! We're having some chocolate cake today!* The dog tried to grab an 'advance' piece of it.

"Behave, d'Artagnan," said Amanda. "You know the rules about chocolate."

On the top of the cake, Régine had written *Welcome to Orvilly, Little Canadian* with butter cream. They all laughed when Amanda read the inscription.

"Thank you so much, both of you. I'll drop by once in a while to say hi, I promise. Come on d'Art."

Paul and Régine helped Amanda to walk outside where a taxi waited for her. The driver put her big suitcase in the trunk. D'Artagnan jumped in the back seat, and Amanda sat on the front passenger seat with Bronx in his box at her feet, and the chocolate cake on her lap. The taxi was full.

The driver started the car. "Hey, your cat looks kind of... weird."

Bronx was staring at the driver, doing one of his scary faces, smashing it against the transparent plastic door, licking it. *Hit the road and drive fast, you idiot. Can't you see that I'm uncomfortable?*

"Oh, don't worry about him," said Amanda. "He often does that to impress people."

"Oh?" answered the cab driver with a worried look.

The car left and Amanda waved to Régine and Paul who stood on the sidewalk in front The Little Norman, waving back at her.

When she stepped into the castle with d'Artagnan and Bronx, Amanda felt different. Different in a good way. She wasn't scared to be there on her own. Well, not exactly on her own, of course. For the first time since she had first entered the castle, she felt at home.

She removed d'Artagnan's leash and put the pet carrier on the floor to free Bronx. The cat left the box quickly, then slowed his pace to look around and inspect the premises.

"Although I have a map of the castle, don't get lost, guys. It might take me a few hours or even a day before I find you."

Sounds like a good plan to me, thought Bronx. *Finally, I'm going to have some space.*

"And I wouldn't want you to starve to death," added Amanda.

D'Artagnan gave a worried look at his friend.

Yikes! I'll keep following you closely then.

Amanda smiled and patted the Great Dane's head. "I was only joking, d'Art."

You never know... thought the dog.

The dog followed Amanda to the kitchen. She put her precious cookbook on the table and looked around her.

"Hey, uh... I'm Amanda, the new owner of the castle."

D'Artagnan wondered who Amanda was talking to.

"Well, I'm not really used to ghosts, but uh... I hope that you and I will get on well, Jeannette." Amanda waited for any sign that would confirm the presence of Jeannette in the room, but nothing happened. "You know, just like you, I love to cook. At least, we have this in common. Right?"

Silence in the room again.

"Well, I hope that you're OK with us sharing this kitchen?"

Amanda startled when she heard several car horns. She recognized the sound of Liliane's Deux Chevaux. D'Artagnan barked. They both ran to the front entrance.

Amanda opened the heavy front door and noticed for the first time the beautiful curls and leaves carved into the old wood. Liliane was parked in front of the door.

"Ready for your makeover, Dame d'Orvilly?"

Amanda chuckled. "Not really," answered Amanda, "but let's go for it." Amanda turned to d'Artagnan. "D'Art, you have to look after the castle for a few hours, please. I'll be back soon. And tonight, there will be a surprise for you. A surprise that involves *food*."

Food? You said the magic word. OK, off you go! I will guard the fortress.

Amanda closed the door, leaving d'Artagnan in the hall. The dog heard a weird sound, and turned around. Bronx was facing him with a threatening look, standing like a tiger protecting his territory, screeching.

Why is this crazy cat looking at me with the smile of a psycho? Wait, nooo!

Bronx jumped on d'Artagnan's back and they started to fight.

The pets were too loud to be able to hear the sound that came from the kitchen. Near a cupboard, whose top doors were open, an old metal tea box had fallen on the floor. A thin white powder had spread on the brown tiles, forming the letters JG.

Chapter 52

Pierre was speechless when he opened his door. Amanda was worried. Should she have ignored Liliane's advice? Did she look like a clown? She felt so uncomfortable in the dress. When was the last time she had worn a dress? In high school maybe, for a party? She wasn't even sure. She always hated wearing dresses. She felt like—

"You look stunning!" exclaimed Pierre.

Amanda looked at him, surprised.

"I do?"

"Yes!"

"You're not making fun of me, right?"

"I wouldn't dare. This dress looks lovely on you."

Amanda smiled. She wore a simple cotton white dress with little green and red embroidered flowers. A light green shawl draped elegantly on her shoulders, and she had cute red flat shoes. After a few trials in the shoe store, Liliane had quickly concluded that Amanda wasn't ready yet for high heels. More training was required.

Pierre took Amanda's hand and invited her to walk up the stairs that lead to his apartment, above the bakery. She kept pushing back her hair, that a hairdresser had curled. They were hanging over her left eye, annoying her. Amanda wasn't used to having her hair free, and even less with curls dancing all around her head.

"Your hair looks great too," said Pierre.

Amanda looked down and smiled. At least, the curls could hide her blushing cheeks.

Then they heard a bark and a screech.

"Oh my God! I forgot them outside!"

Amanda went back down the stairs quickly and opened the door. D'Artagnan was standing on the sidewalk, looking offended, and Bronx was meowing loudly. The carrier box had fallen over on its side.

"Oh my God! I'm really sorry, guys."

Grey clouds suddenly appeared in the sky and rain started to fall on Orvilly-sur-Mer. Amanda ran inside quickly with d'Artagnan, and Pierre took the carrier box.

"You told me that I could bring them with me. Is it still okay?" she asked Pierre. "It's just that I don't want them to spend their first evening alone in the castle."

"No problem, Amanda, I understand," answered Pierre.

The pets were released in the apartment. They started to explore the place.

I'm really getting tired of these moves, complained Bronx, *are we going to settle somewhere steady or what?*

Then the cat smelled something sweet that reminded him of... yes! These choux buns that he had once eaten in the arms of a lady in the bakery.

Bronx ran to a basket full of chouquettes left on a side table. He started to gobble the little pastries covered with sugar. Amanda ran after him.

"Bronx! How many times have I told you not to eat other people's food, it's rude. I'm so sorry Pierre, I feel so embarrassed."

"No worries," said Pierre. "In fact, I prepared these chouquettes for him. I know he loves them."

There you go! I like this guy. Bronx escaped with a little choux bun in his mouth and hid under the sofa.

"Please, have a seat Amanda."

Amanda sat at a round table that Pierre had prepared with great care. It was covered with a spotless ironed white tablecloth, lit by two candles, and a little vase with fresh pink roses was placed in the middle. It looked perfectly romantic.

D'Artagnan walked around the table, unsure where to sit. But he knew one thing: he had to stay close to this table. This apartment smelled of food in a way that promised good meals coming, and he was certainly not going to miss out.

"Pierre, this table looks amazing. Thank you."

"Madam, you deserve to be treated like a queen. I heard what happened at the Village Hall yesterday. Sorry, I couldn't be there. I have to say that I'm impressed. This is a crazy story. So, the mayor, Barbon and the architect really killed Martin Plouque?"

"Yes, they did. But enough about them. I can smell some delicious flavors. May I ask what you've prepared for us tonight?"

The storm rumbled above their heads and the walls trembled. The rain hit the roof louder. They raised their eyes to the ceiling at the same time.

"We'll start with a leek and potato soup to warm us up. Then we'll follow with spaghetti and pesto served with breaded chicken. If your stomach still has room, I'll bring out a cheese plate. As for dessert... let's keep it a surprise for now."

"My turn to be impressed, Pierre. I can't wait to try your food. I'm sure it will be delicious."

Pierre smiled proudly and walked over to the kitchen. He came back with a tray, carrying two hot bowls filled with the creamy soup, and a small basket with pieces of a warm bread he had just baked. He put the bowls on the plates delicately and presented the bread basket to Amanda. "Be careful, the soup is very hot."

Amanda chose a slice. The bread was still warm and smelled divine.

"Oh, by the way, I have a little something for you," said Pierre.

Amanda was intrigued. Pierre took a wrapped gift from a chair nearby and handed it to her.

"A gift? I don't know what to say, Pierre. And I arrived empty handed... I'm so rude. I feel embarrassed."

"Don't be. Just open it."

Pierre smiled, anxious to see Amanda's reaction. She tore the blue paper that wrapped the rectangular gift. Was it a book?

"What's this?"

"Why do people always ask that when they open a gift?" said Pierre. "Open it and you'll see."

Amanda laughed when she saw an old video tape of The Three Musketeers.

"You remembered that I love this movie?"

"Yes. And this is a tape of the 1953 version, the one you prefer, right?" Amanda nodded. "We'll watch it later, if you want?"

"I'd love that, Pierre. But there's one little problem though... Do you have a VCR?"

Pierre laughed.

"Of course not. We'll watch it on TV, from a website." Pierre winked at her.

Amanda felt very lucky. She was melting inside, falling for this incredibly handsome French baker, so delicate and so thoughtful and yet so... virile.

She reviewed her journey from the moment she opened the letter in Victoria, about a month before, announcing the inheritance, until this delightful and romantic moment, sitting with Pierre.

Sure, the weather in Normandy wasn't the most appealing, but Orvilly-sur-Mer was a quaint and lovely village. She had already made new friends, and she was the owner of a castle. A castle! How amazing was that? Soon, she would open her hotel and her fancy restaurant. She was living the French dream. Her French dream.

"May I?" asked Pierre.

Pierre took Amanda's hand which was resting on the table, and kissed it delicately. Amanda smiled and blushed. Her heart was flying high in the sky of Normandy, and she couldn't care less that it was a stormy one.

Hey, wait a minute, what's going on here? D'Artagnan was sitting beside the table, witnessing the scene with indignation.

Hey, you two, I'm still here! And *by the way, I'm starving. I want food too! Fooood! Hello?*

Traditional French Recipes

Cooked By Amanda

Boeuf Bourguignon

Ingredients for 6 servings

For the beef

* 6 oz (180g) of diced bacon
* 1 tablespoon of olive oil
* 3 lb (1.4kg) of stewing beef cut into 2-inch cubes
* 1 sliced carrot
* 1 chopped onion
* 1 tablespoon of flour
* 3 cups of red wine
* 3 cups of beef stock
* 1 tablespoon of tomato paste
* 2 cloves of garlic, minced
* 1/2 teaspoon fresh thyme
* 1 or 2 bay leaves
* Chopped parsley for garnish
* Salt and pepper

For the braised onions

* 20 small white onions, peeled
* 1 1/2 tablespoons of butter
* 1 1/2 tablespoons of olive oil
* 1/2 cup of beef broth
* Salt and pepper

For the sauteed mushrooms

* 1/2 lb (225g) of fresh mushrooms, quartered
* 2 tablespoons of butter
* 1 tablespoon of olive oil

Instructions

1. Preheat your oven to 450°F (230°C).

2. Heat the olive oil in a large dutch oven (or an oven-safe pan). Cook the bacon for a few minutes until it is lightly browned. Remove the bacon from the pan with a slotted spoon and set aside. Don't remove the fat from the pan.

3. Dry the beef using paper towels. Reheat the bacon and saute the beef cubes for a few minutes until the pieces are browned. Remove again with a slotted spoon and set aside.

4. In the same pan, add the carrot and the onion and brown them for few minutes. Pour out the fat, leaving the vegetables in the pan.

5. Add the beef and the bacon and toss them with salt and pepper. Sprinkle the flour over and toss again.

6. Place the pan (uncovered) into the preheated oven for 4 minutes. Toss the meat and return to the oven for 4 more minutes. Remove from the oven and reduce the temperature to 325°F (160°C).

7. Add the wine, stock, tomato paste, garlic and thyme. Bring to a simmer on top of the stove. Cover the pan and return it to the oven. Cook for 3-4 hours, until the meat is fork tender. Meanwhile, prepare the onions and mushrooms.

8. **The braised onions:** heat the butter and the oil in a skillet until it is bubbly. Add the small white onions and cook over medium heat for 10 minutes, roll them around from time to time so they brown evenly. Pour in the beef stock and season with salt and pepper. Bring to a simmer and lower the heat. Cover and simmer for 40-50 minutes. The liquid should evaporate and the onions should brown. Set aside.

9. **The sauteed mushrooms:** heat the butter and oil in a skillet over high heat. Add the mushrooms and cook for about 10 minutes and stir until golden brown. Season with salt and pepper.
10. Once the meat is cooked, pour all the mixture through a sieve. Collect the sauce in a saucepan or a glass bowl and set aside for a few minutes.
11. Return the beef to the pan. Arrange the onions and mushrooms over the meat.
12. Skim fat off the sauce. The sauce should be thick enough to coat a spoon lightly. Pour the sauce over the beef, onions, and mushrooms.
13. You can serve your Beef Bourguignon with boiled potatoes or other vegetables. Enjoy!

Gratin Dauphinois

Ingredients for 6 servings

- 1.65 lb(s) (750g) of potatoes
- 2 cups (1/2 liter) of warm milk
- 1 egg
- 4.4 oz (125g) grated Gruyère
- 3 tablespoons of butter
- A big clove of garlic
- 1/2 teaspoon grated nutmeg
- Salt, pepper

Instructions

1. Pre-heat the oven to 400°F
2. Peel the potatoes and slice them into of 1/8-inch-thick, sprinkle with salt, pepper and grated nutmeg.

3. In a bowl, mix the warm milk and the egg, add salt.
4. Butter a pan and rub it with the garlic clove.
5. Place the slices of potatoes in the pan, forming layers, and add some grated Gruyère in between. Keep some for the last layer on top.
6. Spread the mixture of milk and egg over the pan.
7. Finish by sprinkling the rest of the grated Gruyère and the butter on top.
8. Place in the oven for 40-50 minutes, until the potatoes can be easily pierced with a fork, and the top is brown. Enjoy!

Tarte aux Pommes Normande

Ingredients for 6 servings

For the shortcrust pastry

- 1 egg
- 7 oz (200g) of flour
- 3.5 oz (100g) of caster sugar
- 3.5 oz (100g) of butter
- 1 pinch of salt

For the garnish

- 2.2 lb(s) (1kg) of red apples
- 2 eggs
- 3.5 oz (100g) of caster sugar
- 1.75 oz (50g) of almond powder
- 7 oz (200 ml) of sour cream
- 1/2 liquor glass of Calvados

- 2 tablespoons of chopped almonds

Instructions

1. Make the pastry: beat the egg in a bowl, add the salt and sugar and mix with a wooden spatula. Add the flour and keep stirring until you get the consistency of a shortcrust pastry. Add the butter in small pieces and knead the preparation. The pastry must not stick to your hands. If it does, add a bit of flour.
2. Flatten the pastry with a rolling pin and put it in a buttered and floured pie dish.
3. Preheat your oven at 400°F. Peel the apples and remove the cores. Cut them in thin slices. Place the slices on the pastry by overlapping them a bit. Set aside.
4. In a bowl, beat the eggs, add the sugar, the almond powder, the sour cream, and the Calvados. Spread the mixture on the apples, and add some chopped almonds on top.
5. Bake for 25 minutes.
6. You can eat the pie warm or cold. You can also blaze it up with Calvados. Enjoy!

Feuilletés de Camembert

Ingredients for 1 Camembert puff

- 1 Camembert
- 7 oz (200g) flaky pastry
- 7 oz (200g) smoked bacon, diced
- 1 big onion
- 1 egg
- 1 tablespoon of olive oil

- pepper

Instructions

1. Peel and slice the onion. Brown in a frying pan with some olive oil, then add the dices of smoked bacon. Cook for about 3 minutes, stirring constantly.
2. Cut the Camembert lengthwise in order to have two large slices.
3. Flatten the puff pastry so that it is larger than the Camembert. Put the first slice of Camembert in the center of the pastry.
4. Make regular incisions in the pastry all around the Camembert to get 8 regular strips, going from the slice to the edge of the pastry.
5. Spread the mixture of onion and bacon on the Camembert slice and put the second slice on top of it.
6. Close the Camembert by covering it with the 8 strips of pastry.
7. Turn over the pastry puff and put it on a flat dish to go in the oven.
8. Beat the egg and spread it on top of the pastry puff.
9. Put the puff in the oven at 350°F for 30 minutes.
10. Once cooked, let it rest for 5 minutes and serve with a salad. Enjoy!

Did you like French Cuisine Can Kill You? Then spread the word, write a review!

To be released March 2019, by Rebecca Dunsmuir:

The Mysteries of Orvilly, Book 2
French Weddings Can Kill You

After five months of renovation work, the castle d'Orvilly is finally ready for its grand opening. The hotel inauguration, planned during a weekend, promises to be busy: all the rooms are booked, and prestigious guests are expected, which adds excitement to the event. A couple of French movie stars will get married in the castle, and the wedding media coverage brings journalists and fans to the hotel. All is going well until the bride is found murdered before she can even say "Yes" to the groom. Between demanding guests, eccentric fans, nosy journalists, and a mysterious murder, Amanda and her staff have their hands full. Who killed the famous bride, and why?

Stay in touch!

Visit us at <u>www.manderleybooks.ca</u>

Follow us on Twitter <u>@BooksManderley</u>

Email us at <u>info@manderleybooks.ca</u>

MANDERLEY
BOOKS

About The Author

Rebecca Dunsmuir grew up in Normandy, France, and has been living in Canada for twenty years. She finds delight in writing cozy mysteries as they gather intriguing stories, not so bloody murders, a good dose of humor, a pinch of romance, funny pets who dare to think, ghosts with many secrets to unveil, and characters that you would love to invite for dinner.

Made in the USA
San Bernardino, CA
04 October 2018